Foreign Climes

ALSO BY LUCY FERRISS

A Sister to Honor

The Lost Daughter

Unveiling the Prophet: The Misadventures of a Reluctant Debutante

Nerves of the Heart

The Misconceiver

Sleeping with the Boss: Female Subjectivity and Narrative Pattern in Robert Penn Warren

Against Gravity

The Gated River

Philip's Girl

Foreign Climes

STORIES

Lucy Ferriss

Lucy Ferriss

For Luci,
Hoping you're enjoying
all your climes –
Love,
Lucy
Jan. '22

BRIGHT
HORSE
BOOKS

Brighthorse Books
13202 N River Drive
Omaha, NE 68112
brighthorsebooks.com

ISBN: 978-1-944467-28-9

Author Photo © 2021 Paul John Roberts

"Minnesota" originally appeared in *Michigan Quarterly Review*, "The House of My Other Life" in *American Short Fiction*, "Concorde" in *Foreign Literary*, "Foreign Climes" as "The Difficulty of Translation" in *Michigan Quarterly Review*, "From the Roof" as "Road Rage" in *Roanoke Review*, "Sunset District" as "In the Sunset" in *Missouri Review*, material from "The Garage" in *A Sister to Honor*, "The Difficulty of Translation" in *Crossing Borders*, and "Old Man" in *Shenandoah*.

For permission to reproduce selections from this book, contact the editors at info@brighthorsebooks.com. Visit us on the web at brighthorsebooks.com. Brighthorse books are distributed to the trade through Ingram Book Group and its distribution partners.

For my sons, who brave new worlds

Wherever you go, go with all your heart.
—*The Analects of Confucius*

CONTENTS

Foreign Climes

Minnesota

FINALLY, WHEN I WAS ELEVEN, I got to meet my mom's lover. She and I had flown into Palm Springs. I was a tennis player, and by a series of lucky breaks I had made it to the Easter Bowl. If you had asked me, I would have said I had not slept in a week. Every moment called for a state of high alert. I patted my chest sometimes, or my thighs, to be sure they still belonged to me, the boy who was going to national competition.

"Now, don't be overconfident," my dad told me before we left, which was his way of telling me I sucked.

Palm Springs rushed up at us out of the desert, like a city in a pop-up book. We lived then in North Carolina, and I had never imagined landscape like this—so many shades of brown, mountains pushing like giant pimples out of the skin of the bare land. Then we were on the ground, among the white buildings and bright billboards and palm trees. I figured that we had come into money, or something like money.

The hotel was in the shape of a star. Its rays, which the lady at the desk called "pods," were named for Indian tribes. The center of the star was a huge oval swimming pool with little side pools like moons—a jacuzzi, a kiddie pool, a fountain. The minute we set our bags down in our room, I ran to explore. "Can you remember our room number?" my mom asked, pushing off her sandals.

"Apache two sixty-six," I said.

"Then you may explore by yourself. If you get lost, ask a person in a uniform to help you find your way back. I'm tired," she said. She smiled with the light in her eyes that told me how glad she was to have an energetic son. "I'm going to shower," she said, "and buff my nails."

"Sure," I said, as if she'd made a joke.

My mom was neither a beautiful nor a plain woman to me. She carried my tennis bag and bought me sports drinks. When I looked up from the tennis court after a good point, she was looking down from the bleachers, smiling without showing her teeth, which were large and very white. She wore tennis shoes to my matches in case I needed her to warm me up on the court, though she never hit hard enough to satisfy me. Her fingernails were her own business. My dad laughed the rare times she tried to prettify herself, coloring her hair or plucking her eyebrows, which were heavy and highly arched. "Dress it up and call it crème brulée," he said, "it's still pudding to me." Then he'd lick his lips and say, "Don't get me wrong about pudding."

But when she came to find me, watching a pair of eighteen-year-olds on the hotel's tennis court, my mom's nails glistened coral, matching the gloss she'd applied to her lips. In the desert air she looked dewy. "Those boys are good," she said, perching next to me. We were both jet-lagged, though I didn't recognize the symptoms at the time. The air sucked the moisture from my skin. The sun seemed out of place, insisting on its right to bear down. My throat was parched.

"That's Rajiv Deglani," I whispered back. "He's number two in eighteens!"

"Well, he's very good," she repeated. She never spoke softly enough, next to the court. Rajiv, switching sides, glanced our way. "Do you want something to drink?" she asked me.

"Ssh," I said.

Rajiv bounced the ball three times, stared at it a moment, then tossed it up for the serve. For a second it blocked the sun. That was Rajiv's superstition, I figured, the bouncing and staring. Mine was to tap my right toe twice against the service line. When I received a serve, I tapped both toes and spun my racquet. My mom had complained that I was going through shoes for no good reason but toe-tapping. This was partly a joking complaint, because she was proud of how well I played tennis, but once or twice I'd caught her staring hard at the holes worn through the toes of an otherwise excellent pair of K-Swiss. She shook her head slowly, an unbeliever, before she dropped the useless things in the trash.

Rajiv's serve had a lot of kick, but the guy on the other side managed to return it cross-court and get in position for Rajiv's backhand slice, which held in the air a second before dropping just inside the baseline. Then the guy drove it down the line. Rajiv's forehand return was a soft lob that the guy caught at midcourt and slammed to the ad side. The ball bounced over the fence and skittered underneath a thorny bush. I scurried down from the bleachers and retrieved it.

"Thanks, bud," said Rajiv.

"Is he here for the tournament?" my mom asked me when I got back to the bleacher.

"Mom. He's *eighteen*."

"So? He's a junior."

"The eighteens are in Alabama this year, and they're next week. I think he's here for his brother," I said. I didn't bother with the rest, how Sandeep Deglani was ranked number 15 in the country even though he'd just turned eleven. My mom was glad for me to do well, but the way the system worked was a mystery to her.

We watched Rajiv for a while. He lost the first set in a tie-break, and then he and his opponent wasted time by the net. My mom announced that she for one could use a drink.

"I want to play putt putt," I said.

"It's nine o'clock our time, Jimmy. You check in at eight tomorrow morning."

"So? That's eleven o'clock our time. I'm not tired."

"We should eat something," she said firmly, and at that I was hungry.

About two years before, I'd put my foot down on kiddie meals. They were boring and not enough food, and I was too old for plastic toys. Since then, my mom ordered a glass of wine

15

for herself and a meal for me. I usually asked for the calamari appetizer as well. She nibbled on bread while I destroyed the calamari, then halfway through my baked ziti I would be full, and she would dispatch the rest.

We settled at a table on the veranda. The rest of our time in Palm Springs, my mom pointed out, we would be eating elsewhere. But just for tonight, because we were tired, we could eat at the hotel. I nodded and checked out the menu, which wasn't promising. Too much written in Italian, and too many cream sauces. It occurred to me that my mom was saving money by buying just one grown-up meal. If I had gone along with the kiddie-meal idea, she might have ordered exactly what it was she wanted—the grilled fresh tuna, for instance, or the ratatouille. But none of the other boys on the tour ordered kiddie meals. Their parents ordered a regular meal for the kid and regular meals for themselves and let the waitress clear half-full plates from their table, no regrets.

I ordered calamari; my mom got her wine. "The air's getting cold," I complained.

"That's the desert," she said, and right then her lover walked out onto the veranda.

"Cynthia," he said.

If I'd been a dog, my ears would have gone up. Everyone else called her Cindy.

"Lookie who's here," she said.

"Mind if I join you?" he said.

He wasn't good-looking. He was heavyset and had a goatee. His laugh was choked-off and nervous, *heh heh*. He stuck out his hand. "Jimmy D," he greeted me.

I pulled my hand, a dead animal, out from under the tablecloth. Jimmy D was my tennis name. The other boys yelled it when they were cheering for me. My mom yelled it when she got really excited. But my dad called me Jim, and so did my sister who was in kindergarten. I liked the nickname right up to the moment it came out of my mom's lover's mouth.

"I'm Drew," he said, taking the dead animal in his wide palm. "I'm a friend of your mother's, from way back. She told me you were coming out this way, and I thought, 'Why not see Cynthia and her big tennis guy?'"

"Hi," I said. "Mom, do they have marinara sauce?"

"I'm sure they do, honey," she said. It was like a clarinet was playing deep in her throat. "Drew, join us." He'd already sat down. "How's your room?"

"I've told them I resent being a Pawnee," he said with a *heh heh*. "Otherwise it's all right." He picked up my mom's menu, glanced for about three seconds, then folded it up. "Jimmy D," he said, sizing me up. "You need some real food."

"Tell them ziti with marinara, if they have it," I said to my mom.

"You like Mexican?" he asked me.

"My name's Jim," I told him.

He nodded. "Tacos, fajitas, you like those?"

"Sure."

"We'll get you out of here tomorrow, Jim, feed you good." He said this with his lips pulled back, as if he were going to eat me himself. As he settled into his chair, his knee bumped against my mom's. I could tell from the way both their bodies did a little jerk.

"What are you ordering, Cynthia?" he said.

"Oh. You know," she said, and gestured at the wine.

"Growing girl like you. The lady will have the scampi," Drew said to the waitress, "and I'll have prime rib. Rare. Pawnee 106, the whole tab."

"We'll waste food," I said to my mom.

"Shush," she said. "Enjoy it."

After supper they left me in the game room. Some kids I knew had arrived—the number 18 from Texas and the number 25 from New York, both of them seeded for this tournament—and we played Mortal Kombat and pinball. The number 18 said this kid Jason had hooked him in Phoenix last month, and the

25 and I said we'd met up with Jason before, he was a cheater all right. We compared birthdays—the 25, who was a chunky Chinese kid, was aging up the next month, but the 18 and I were both in the twelves though winter. "Want to do doubles with me at the Copper Bowl?" I asked him. "My partner Ryan aged up last month."

It was a risky question, because I was ranked 31, but he said, "Might could. My partner's movin' back to Spain."

This was great news for me. I was good at doubles, because I was tall for my age and I attacked the net. All I needed was a decent partner. These guys in the game room with me, acting like normal guys, were the best players in the country. Now one of them would be my doubles partner. Mine! I ran back to Apache 266 to tell my mom.

She had stopped in—her pocketbook was sitting on the nightstand—but she wasn't there and she hadn't left a note. I chose my bed and started flipping channels. I told myself she had gone for a walk. She often did that, when we stayed at a hotel. She said watching me exercise all day gave her nervous exhaustion. She found the weirdest places to walk—gullies that ran behind the hotels and ended up in dilapidated parks, or paths that followed run-off creeks and took her the other side of the highway. I worried about her a little. That is, I worried that she'd get lost or kidnapped, and I'd have no one to drive me to the tournament site. My dad thought the whole junior tennis tour was a bad idea, so he would never come fetch me and take me to my match, if my mom wandered off.

I flipped among *South Park*, *Six Feet Under*, and an HBO movie with Harrison Ford. My head ached. I thought my mom ought to get back and bug me to go to bed. I pictured myself playing at the Copper Bowl with the number 18 kid; I pictured his cross-court forehand setting me up for a sweet overhead. I wanted to tell her about it, and I was mad that she wasn't there. I thought what my dad would say if I lost his wife.

Back home, an older girl lived next door—with both her

parents at first, and then, starting the year before, with just her dad. When I asked about her mom, she said, "Oh, my mom has a lover now," as if a lover was something that mothers acquired at some point in their development, the way you got braces in middle school or a driver's license when you turned 16.

Sometimes, when my parents fought, my mom got this distant, curious look in her eyes. It looked as if she were watching a movie, or as if she had gone for one of those walks in her head, and might not come back. When I had met Drew Heilbrun at dinner, I'd known right off that he was the answer. I just hadn't got the question straight yet.

At ten-thirty, I called her cell phone. This was something I was supposed to do only in emergencies, since the hotel charged us a minor fortune to call long-distance and calling the cell was long-distance even if she was down in the lobby. But it didn't matter because she didn't pick up. Ten minutes later I heard her card slide into the lock.

"Hey," she whispered, as if someone in the room were asleep.

"Where were you?" I said in my normal voice.

"I don't know. Just out," she said.

"The guy who's ranked 18 is going to be my doubles partner," I said.

"That's great," she said. Normally, she would gone on to ask who number 18 was, where she might have seen him play, how Ryan would feel if I kept playing with this other boy when we all aged up. Then she'd have congratulated me on being such a social genius. That was what she called me, because I got on well with people; she thought of herself as shy.

But all she said was, "Look at the moon."

I sat up straighter in the bed and looked at my mother, standing by the hotel window. I felt how she was no longer there—in that hotel, in Palm Springs—totally on my account. Something else was drawing her away. My superstition kicked in: if her attention was divided, I would lose in the tournament.

Reading my thoughts, she turned away from the moon and

pretended to be the mother she'd been a few hours before. "I wonder who you'll meet in your first match," she said, sitting on her bed and pulling off her sandals.

"I'll be seeded, I think." This was what I usually said, that summer anyway. Before, I would say, "I hope I won't get a seeded kid." The seeds got easy first rounds, though there was always the chance of an upset. My mom used to remind me of that chance, when I had to play a seed. Now that I was seeded, my dad reminded me of it.

"You need a good night's sleep, though," my mom said.

"Whatever," I said. I flipped through the channels. I didn't want to look at her.

"Teeth," she said.

"Whatever," I said.

Usually, when I tested her, she took away the remote and flicked off the TV. This time she just sighed, as if my disobedience were ivy that kept growing back. Then she pulled her nightgown from the dresser drawer and went to the bathroom to change. She sang to herself in the bathroom. This wasn't unusual. She crooned old Broadway show tunes in the shower; she hummed while she was putting stuff on her face. This time, though, the song seemed dopey. I swung my legs off the brocaded bedspread and marched to the bathroom door, which was ajar.

"Please stop that," I said. "You're keeping me awake."

"Why, Jimmy," she said. She tipped her head at me, puzzled. Her face was white with cream. "You were just watching TV," she said.

"I'm not watching now," I said. "I am trying to sleep. I have to play tennis early in the morning."

She pinched her lips together, the lips looking very pink in her white face. "Brush your teeth, then," she said. She stepped back from the beige vanity where she had laid out my Star Wars toothpaste and brush. I looked at them, then at her.

"Goodnight," I said. I went back to the bed, flicked off the TV, and shut off the light. I lay there trembling. If you had asked me, I would have said they put the air conditioning on too high. My mother began to hum again, softer this time, a different melody.

•

I LIKED MY DRAW VERY MUCH. I ran to see it the next morning while my mom was getting take-out breakfast from a long line in the hotel lobby. The tournament desk was set up in a hut back of the hotel, behind the Pequot pod. Below, the courts fanned out under the clean sun. In the distance, the mountains that had looked like pimples lifted out of the desert, so alive you thought they might start advancing on you.

I was playing a nothing kid from Minnesota in my first round. Minnesota! You could barely find the place on a map, much less play tennis there. Once I beat him, I'd be up against Austin Chalfant, from Florida, who thought he was hot because he was big, but he'd never broken the top hundred in the nation. Beating him, I'd face the chunky number 25 guy I'd talked to last night. If I beat him—and this was a big if—I would be in the quarter-finals against Sandeep Deglani. My ranking would shoot up to the top two dozen in the whole country.

"Way to fix it, Jimmy D." This was number 18, leaning over my shoulder to see the draw.

"Who've you got?" I checked the list, mostly because I'd forgotten his name. There it was, in the other half of the bracket: Conor Grady, 18.

"Some Yankee." Conor grinned at me. "We'll be nice to them, huh?"

"Nice as we can," I said.

Conor was a tall, freckled boy with braces and a white baseball cap. I'd watched him play. He wasn't a pusher, but he had a nice baseline game, with a one-handed backhand that bulleted down the line to the corner. My mom said once that he must have drilled that shot a million times. I didn't like to drill shots.

"Well, break a leg," Conor said.

My mom was at the front of the breakfast line. Next to her

was her lover. I'd come running between the Indian pods and around the pool and its moons to give her the good news about the draw. I had forgotten how I'd felt the night before. Next to my mom, Drew looked solid and sort of flat-headed. My dad was tall; his head was narrow, with a rat's nest of hair that he left long on top like Lyle Lovett. Everyone said I looked like him, but I kept my hair under a baseball cap.

"Honey Nut Cheerios," said my mom when she saw me. "Eat up. They're his favorite," she said to Drew, "but I won't keep them in the cupboard."

"What a mean lady," Drew said, and winked at me.

"I'd rather have Rice Krispies," I said.

She looked at me funny, her dark eyebrows lifting up. "Go trade it in, then," she said. "They won't care, if you haven't opened the box."

I considered opening the box, but something about my mom's lover—his bulk, or the set of his mouth under the facial hair—gave me pause.

"How's your draw, Jim?" Drew said when we were sitting at a tiny round table.

"Okay," I said. I dug into the Krispies.

"Must feel good to be seeded," he said.

"Whatever," I said into my bowl.

"Is it okay if I watch your match?"

I shrugged. The matches were open to the public. Usually my opponent had his coach and both his parents and a bunch of kids from his club rooting for him, and I had my mom.

It wasn't that my dad was a terrible parent. He just didn't believe there was anything an eleven-year-old boy could do that would warrant laying out thousands of dollars a year and traveling hundreds of miles. When he was eleven he played pick-up basketball with his brothers and a couple of kids on the street, and he was happy.

"I am glad to know," my mom said to him once, "that you were a happy child."

By which she meant that he was not a happy grown-up.

"I've got to check in," I said, not answering Drew's question.

"You haven't finished your cereal," my mom said.

The Krispies looked like bleached rat turds floating in milk. "I'm not hungry," I said, and hoisted my case.

•

OUTSIDE, THE SKY WAS HAZY. The hairs on my legs stood out in the cool air. The Minnesota kid was named Spence. "Spence!" I muttered to myself after we'd cracked the balls open and gone to the baseline. No one would be caught dead on the pro tour with a name like Spence. Andre maybe, but not Spence. I decided to think of him as Minnesota. *Min-neh-soh-ta*. I'd play a whole state.

Minnesota warmed up okay—Western grip, two-fisted backhand, deep on the cross-courts. His overheads were weak. His serve was meant to have a kick in it, but really all it did was twist to the forehand. If I set up right, I could put it away down the line, and we would have a quick match.

"What's your ranking?" he asked after I'd spun the racquet.

"Thirty-one," I said. "I'm a seed."

"Oh, yeah?" he said. "I didn't notice."

I rolled my eyes in my mom's direction, to clue her that I was playing an ignoramus. She was sitting the way she always did—a little apart from the other parents, with her straw hat shading her face, a Nestea can on the ground next to her, and a book on her lap. When I started playing she would put the book away. At changeovers she would take it out and read a page.

"You play *long* matches, Jim," she had told me. "A girl needs a little distraction."

When I rolled my eyes, she glanced up. She gave me what she called her Mona Lisa smile, just the corners of her mouth lifting.

I won the toss and served. My first two serves were straight, hard overheads that jumped off the green surface. Minnesota got his racquet on each of them and sent the ball sailing, first into the other court, then into the fence. I was pumped. Usually, in the twelves, whoever got the serve in the first round of the tournament lost it out of nerves. We all should have chosen to receive, but nobody even considered that. Did Roger Federer choose to receive? Did Novak?

I'd set up to serve at 30 love when a let ball rolled on from the next court. Conor Grady was there, in his second set already, up three zip. I knocked it back. "Thanks," he said. When I turned back to pick up my own ball, I saw my mom's lover, standing behind and just to her left. He lifted his hand and waved his fingers. I shifted my gaze to my mom, stuck in the Mona Lisa smile. Then I double faulted. Double faulted again. At thirty all, I got my second serve over, but without much kick in it, and Minnesota lobbed back with enough topspin that he kept me far back of the baseline until he dropped a wimpy little shot over the net.

I looked at my mom. The smile was gone. Something worse had taken its place. Her right arm came across her chest and up to her left shoulder, where her right hand lay on Drew Heilbrun's. You could see the coral nail polish, reflecting the sun.

I tapped my toe twice against the service line and served hard. The return popped up. I moved in for the overhead, and bombed it into the net. Game, Minnesota.

As we traded sides, I glared at my mom. She'd brought her hand back down, and reinstalled the smile. The straw hat shaded her eyes from the sun, which was already burning away haze. We weren't allowed to talk to each other, but I had always figured that moms and sons had telepathy between them. This time I telepathed, *Get him out of here*. She gave me a thumb up.

I took the next game, but it wasn't pretty. At deuce, Minnesota had served weak to my backhand, and I drove the return cross-court so that all he could do—and it surprised me that he got to it—was to lob the ball deep with plenty of topspin. It hit and I dropped the head of my racquet. I held up my index finger. Out.

"Are you sure?" asked Minnesota.

"Positive," I said. We were playing hard court, so it didn't matter, but I pointed my racquet at an invisible mark. "Couple inches," I said.

He shrugged. His shoulders looked thin. On the other side of the bench from my mom, his mom and dad were both shaking their heads. I didn't look at my mom. I heard her explaining—too loudly—how it was Jimmy's call and the other boy could get the official if he wanted, but basically you went by the honor system.

I tapped my toes and twisted my racquet. Minnesota's next serve was wobbly; I chipped and charged, and put the volley away. My mom's lover clapped. "Good game!" he called.

Which you were allowed to do. Which was what my opponents' parents and coaches and neighbors were always doing, and I was jealous. I managed to remind myself of this fact as I bounced the yellow ball. Only—and now I was tossing to serve at one all—you didn't shout "Good game!" when your guy had just hooked the other guy.

I double faulted. That was three times in two service games. "Shit!" I yelled.

"Let." This was Conor, on the next court. He'd been about to volley, and caught the ball. He looked at me.

"Sorry," I said.

He shrugged, and went back to his baseline. I went back to mine, and proceeded to lose the game.

You got ninety seconds for changeovers. I threw my racquet into the net, sagged into the plastic chair, uncorked my thermos, and shot venom at my mom. She was deep in conversation with Drew Heilbrun, explaining to him everything that was weird about me. He kept nodding his shaggy head. Last night he had told me he'd run high-school track, but in shorts and a T-shirt he looked really out of shape. He was an architect, my mom had said. Big whoop, I thought. My dad sold insurance.

When I lost the first point of the next game on an unforced error, I retrieved the ball and slammed it over to Minnesota. He caught it off the fence and walked up to the service line. "You can get cited for that," he said.

"Shut up and serve," I said.

Three points later, I did get cited. At deuce, I'd hit a sweet down-the-line shot on the ad side. Minnesota chased it down and missed it. "Out!" he shouted.

"Are you kidding me?" I said, approaching the net. "That was no way wide."

"I didn't say it was wide," he said. "It was deep, actually."

"Oh yeah, right."

"It was deep," he said. He gestured with his racquet as if at a mark.

"Hard court," I said. "There aren't any marks. That ball was good and you know it."

"It was deep, Jimmy."

"Cheater."

"It's my call."

I turned away. I remembered my arm swinging, just a hair too much force on the topspin, enough to place it past the baseline. He'd been out of position; I'd had the whole court to place the ball in. I wanted to look at my mom, but I knew what I'd see—Drew, by now on the bench next to her, elbows on his knees, squinting in the sun. I shut my eyes. "Fuck," I said.

"Point penalty," said the official. "Audible obscenity."

I hadn't even noticed her sneaking up. I bit my lower lip. Inside my mouth I could taste the blood. Minnesota tossed the balls over the net to me and changed the score cards on the side of the net. Three to one.

My mom used to tell me that when she saw me getting myself into a hole, she pictured it like a well, with me at the bottom of it and her hand on the crank for the bucket. She would lower the bucket into the well, she said, and so long as I would get into the bucket she had the strength to crank me back up. Plenty of times I'd pictured this when I was playing badly. I'd tell myself just to get into that bucket, and then I'd feel my mom's whole focus, her whole self, winding the rope around the winch until I saw daylight.

This time, though, I wasn't getting into the fucking bucket. Let her figure something else out, I thought, and I lost the next two games. Then I held serve and—finally—broke Minnesota. I was serving against the set, three five. At the changeover I allowed myself a glance in her direction, and she gave me two thumbs up. The problem was that her lover, like some kind of monkey, stuck his two fat thumbs up as well.

I don't know what happens to other people when they encounter their parent's lover for the first time. I never asked that girl next door. For me, as I bounced the ball at the baseline, I was no longer on the court at all. I was back home in Charlotte. In the family room, to be exact, where we had a yard-sale bumper pool table and a decrepit bar that my kid sister used as a launching pad. I was watching TV. At supper my parents had gotten into one of those arguments you tune out. It didn't have to do with me specifically. It had to do with wanting more than you were allowed to get. When they'd run out of stuff to say my mom went up to their bedroom to make a phone call. I'd hopped up from my bean bag, stood on the sagging bar, tilted my head and craned my neck. She had talked on the phone a long time. Gradually her voice had gone from the tight holding-back of tears to a musical lilt, and she'd even laughed once. I hadn't made out words. But now, as I readied my serve, I was sure she had been talking to this guy, this Drew Heilbrun, who sat so solidly next to her on the bench. That had been a year ago, that time in the family room.

I don't even know where the serves went.

Then I was back in the game. I was talking to myself. Everybody did it. "Come on, Jimmy D, come on," I said. "Let's win this. No more errors. This is easy now, let's do this. First serve, first serve!"

I got my second serve in and took the point, but I didn't like it. I whapped the bottom of my shoe with the racquet. "First serve!" I said again.

"Let's go, Jimmy D!" said my mom, and she clapped her hands three times. This was normally a great thing for her to do.

When the overhead came, I was in perfect position—mid-court, index pointing, shoulders turned. A ball from Conor's court dribbled by the net, but I saw it only out of the corner of my eye, and I wasn't going to give up this chance for a smash. I swung and whiffed.

"Let!" I cried as the ball bounced behind me. I looked around for Conor's ball, which had rolled to the gate. "Let! Let!"

"You can't call a let ball after you've missed the point," said Minnesota.

"Let!" I said again, as if this was some word a kid from Minnesota didn't understand.

"You can't—"

"I *know* the rules," I said. I dropped my racquet and kicked it into the net.

This time the official was just outside the gate, near my mom and her lover. "Racquet abuse," she called. "Game penalty. What was the score?"

"Five three," said Minnesota. "Me."

"That's the set, then," she said. "Take ninety seconds before the second set."

Fire roared in my head. I sat on the plastic chair. A drink of water might have put out the fire, but I wasn't going to take a drink of water. Minnesota sat in his chair and uncorked a fresh Gatorade. Behind me, Conor won his game. "Jimmy D," he said.

"Yeah," I said.

I thought he was going to say something nice, but he said, "I think we better forget that old doubles thang."

"Okay," I said.

I looked up. The whole world, it seemed to me, was on fire. The only thing not burning was my mom. She had stood up from the bench and was talking to her lover, explaining, softly this time. She glanced over at me. At hip level she gave me her fist sign, the hold-steady sign. I thought maybe she could handle even this—this awful display of her awful kid to her lard-belly lover. But boy, she should see what I'd do next. I would burn the court up, that's what I'd do. Then see what old Drew thought of me. Just see.

She spoke to him again. They both wiggled their fingers at me, and walked away.

"C'mon," said Minnesota. "It's been ninety seconds. You don't want to get defaulted."

"Shut up," I said to him.

I took a swig from my cooler. My mom had stuffed it with ice from the hotel so it was chilly as spring water. I picked up my racquet and went out to the baseline to receive.

I took the second set six to one. At the split we got ten minutes' break. I pulled a dollar from my racquet case and bought a Gatorade, then walked over a couple of courts and watched Austin Chalfant, who was pouring sweat but winning five three in the first. "Go, Austin!" I shouted, and he grinned at me like a big shark. Starting back to my court, I looked for my mom. I wouldn't have admitted it, but she was what I was scanning for—up one walkway, along the other. "Good," I muttered to myself. "Get lost."

Back on my court, heading out for the last set, Minnesota squared his thin shoulders and waved at his coach. On his baseball cap, he'd sewn little decals, for 4H Club and his basketball team and the Timberwolves. I had no mercy for him. By the time it was four love, the whole state of Minnesota was at courtside, screaming. "Bring it back, Spence!" "You can do it, Spence!" "It's all you, Spence!" "Don't let him take you, Spence!" When the official planted herself by the net, hoping to catch me, I returned serves that were two inches long. Then I moved in to net and put the ball away. Five love. On the changeover, Minnesota wiped his eyes, but he didn't break.

At forty love in the last game, I approached the net. I held out my hand. Minnesota, pale and sweating, stared at me. "What are you doing?"

"Congratulations," I said.

"You're forfeiting?"

"Good luck in the next round."

"What the hell's wrong with you?"

Courtside, the Minnesotans were going nuts. His hand, when I shook it, felt like all the bones had melted out of it.

They still had pay phones then; I wasn't allowed a cell phone. I found one and called my dad collect. "I'm giving it up," I said.

"Good for you," he said.

"On one condition," I said.

"Hey," he said. "No conditions."

I set down the phone. Make her give him up, I'd been going to say. At the tournament desk I formally withdrew. I left my case there and walked along the gravel path, past the entrance to the courts and the mini golf, past the parking lot, to a broad road outside and, across it, a few houses and shops. This was what my mom saw, I thought, when she walked away from the hotels and into her life. Beyond the shops the land rose to what looked like a flat knoll. I hopped across at a break in the traffic. I followed a small road that turned to dirt, then walked that until I couldn't get any higher. My throat stuck to itself with dried spit. From a rock where a lizard had been basking, I looked across the desert.

Beyond the palm trees and fat buildings of Palm Springs, the hardpan spread out in varying shades of dust. Farther off, the mountains moved. There were no shadows anywhere. The things that lived out there were fast and good at hiding. How weird it was, I thought, that people were living in the middle of this. Sitting in restaurants, jumping into swimming pools, playing tennis, having sex. I added that last one, because I meant to make myself see my mom and her lover. But I didn't know how to arrange them. In a little while, I walked back down.

The Garage

Gus's CONVERTED GARAGE reminded Afia of the quarters occupied by Tayyab, the cook, back in Nasirabad. It was tucked the same way, behind a hedge at the end of a driveway, with a tiny, nailed-up porch and a side door. Only Tayyab had a whole family in his quarters—separated by curtains for various privacies—while Gus's was one big room with a portable radiator cranking electric heat.

"They are like swimming jewels," she said of the fish in the big tank set up at the far end of the garage. She had never known a person to keep tropical fish. The snake and lizard—their cages by the adjacent wall, complete with heat lamps—reminded her of what anyone might see in the hotter area of her province, down by Peshawar. And the two cats reminded her of Nasirabad, where cats roamed free. Only these bright swimmers, some of them translucent, their eyes unblinking, mesmerized her.

"They exhibit different behaviors," Gus said, standing close behind her, his hand on her shoulder. "See how the betta come up to gulp air? And this little suckermouth hides—see her behind the castle?"

"You always say 'her.'"

"Yeah, they all seem like girls to me. I don't know why."

In a week, she would leave for Nasirabad. Gus kept saying it was not a big deal. That he would miss her for the three weeks, sure, but he would be busy with vet-school applications and his own family in Pittsfield, and he would write her every day. She didn't know about getting email in her village, she'd reminded him. There was Ali Bhai's, the internet café, but otherwise not much of a signal. "Anyway," she'd said, "I can't be writing while

I am home. It is"—she wanted to say *dangerous*, but then he would ask how it could be dangerous, which was not possible to explain here—"It's weird," she said.

He'd seized on this news about the internet to calm her down. Last week a photo of Afia had appeared on the college website, celebrating Diversity Day. She had freaked out. Her brother, Shahid, who had brought her here in the first place, had stormed into her room, demanding and demanding. Who belonged to the hand at the edge of the picture? Did she want him to ship her back home, covered in shame? What if their Baba saw this image? She had wept and shaken her head, swearing her *namus* was intact, she would not cause shame to Shahid lala. Only when Gus reminded her that her family back home could not access this web page did she calm down. The next time Shahid started badgering her, Gus was in her heart and she acted brave. It was only a photo, she told Shahid, and she was doing nothing wrong in it, she didn't even remember this guy he kept talking about, and who was he to go on like that, about *ghairat* and *namus*, honor and shame, he wasn't Baba. Everyone had been holding hands on Diversity Day.

She turned away from the fish tank to Gus's little stove—two burners below a microwave—where she was making him a special tikka, the first time she had cooked for him. She didn't like the yoghurt she'd found for the marinade—they were too thick, the yoghurts in America, and they lacked the tang you needed for a good lassi. But she'd managed to find a heavy iron skillet at the Salvation Army, and they'd opened the high windows behind the stove to let the smoke escape.

She knew from TV how cooking was part of courtship in America. The men and women advanced their intimacy to where they were playing house, making the roles that would become tedious into moments of romance—candles; a tiny white apron untied to reveal a clingy top; the masculine uncorking of wine. She and Shahid sometimes watched these shows broadcast from Peshawar, and Baba would come in and laugh

33

at the man who thought his life would forever be this way: his perfumed lady staring longingly at him over roast chicken. *It is an illness they suffer from*, he would say, *and when they recover they find themselves married*.

She was ill, she supposed. Odd feelings came over her at unexpected moments. Sometimes, it seemed her skin was not strong enough to contain the energy of her body. Other times her breath would not come right, and then it was as if she didn't even need to breathe, as if her feelings for Gus drew oxygen from the air and charged her blood.

He'd put on a song track they both liked, Rufus Wainwright, and fed the cats, and now he came to stand behind her. "Smells nice," he said, nuzzling her ear.

"The tikka, or my hair?" she asked. Because she no longer covered, now, when she was alone with him, and her thick hair curled down her shoulders. He didn't answer but wrapped his arms around her waist, and he moved with her as she chopped the onions and tasted the sauce. "Don't want to hold you and feel so helpless," he sang along with the song. "Don't want to smell you and lose my senses."

The girls Afia lived with in the dorm fell in and out of love with boys and with each other every day. They talked about birth control the way they talked about food—natural versus organic, controlling what they put in their bodies. When they could have been unlocking the secrets of proteins, they were weeping in the shower or giggling on their phones. It was as Baba had said, a disease. But for her first nine months in America, Afia had been immune. Even when she went to watch Shahid play squash, even when he introduced her to the guys on his team, she paid no attention to any of them, certainly not to the freckly redhead at the bottom of the lineup.

Then in September she'd gone to a med school fair with Taylor, who sometimes talked, idly, of becoming a pediatrician. Forty-five American med schools were there with their pamphlets and computer videos set up on plastic-covered folding tables; and five veterinary schools in a corner by the auditorium stage. When Taylor spotted Gus by himself at the table for Tufts, she gave a little squeal. "He's that cutie from your brother's team," she'd said. "Poor lonely boy. Come on."

He reminded her, that day, of the village boys, the way they could prattle about goats or the weather but fell back to mumbling if asked about their sisters or their homes. Gus said he didn't have any sisters or brothers. He grimaced when Taylor called him a jock. You can play squash by yourself, he said; that's how he'd started, when he was a puny kid and didn't get picked for any high school teams. "You're not puny now," Taylor had said, and Afia had felt herself blushing, because her eyes had fallen on his shoulders, the way they pulled at his T-shirt. He was interested in endangered species, he'd said. He thought he might be a vet at a zoo, or go somewhere exotic like Africa. Only it was hard, to get into vet school. Maybe he shouldn't play so much squash, Afia had suggested. He should be studying. That was not, he'd said, the advice her brother gave him when they roomed together. "When was that?" she'd asked, surprised.

"Frosh year," he'd said. And all Shahid talked about, back then, was squash and his brilliant sister, the one he wanted to bring to the States to study medicine. "He missed you bad," Gus said, and Afia felt her face grow warm.

It had been Taylor's idea to haul him out for pizza. When Taylor got bored with his short answers about the fraternity scene, Afia managed to lift her voice and ask him what exotic species interested him most. "Reptiles," he said. He went on to describe what had been happening to habitats in the Amazon and sub-Saharan Africa. He told her about Pearl his corn snake and Voltaire the iguana. He described the fish he'd acquired, saying that before medicine began obsessing him, he'd thought of becoming a marine biologist. Eventually, the pizza cold and her beer finished, Taylor told Afia she was going to roll, off to meet her boyfriend at an Amherst party. Gus offered to give Afia a lift home.

35

No, she'd said when he'd asked if he could see her again. She did not date, she said. He promised not to touch her, he understood things were different for her. He liked her, that was all. He liked talking to her. What time was it, by then? Three a.m., they remembered later. They had spent most of it in his car, their breath steaming the windows, the air still warm back then, late summer crickets singing. She had told him things she'd never told anyone, not even her mother. About her rebellious friend, Lema, back in Nasirabad. About her stepbrother Khalid who frightened her. About her fears of the drone strikes in the mountains and what would happen to her sisters Sobia and Muska, would Baba ever let the family leave?

They could talk again, she said. Which they did three nights later, under a full moon by the river. The next week on a hike in Huntington. On Columbus Day they'd gone apple-picking with Afia's roommates, who kept calling them a cute couple. Afterwards they'd come back to this garage, where he'd introduced her to his pets. By Halloween she'd let Pearl wrap around her arm. That same week she had bumped into Gus in the hallway outside the squash center when she was on her way to the lavatory, and there in that public place he had leaned into her and planted his lips on her own. All that evening her lips had buzzed. Sometime late he had called on the dorm phone. *I have feelings for you, I can't help it, I do* he'd said, and she'd said without thinking, *I do too, for you I mean.*

Now, cooking in the garage he called home, she shooed him away and flamed the tikka. The cats—Facebook and Ebay, he'd named them—meowed and rubbed at her legs even as smoke billowed up and drifted out the high windows. On her instructions, he ran the blender to make a version of lassi that wasn't the same as home but would have to do. They sat at his rickety folding table and ate. On the iPod, Rufus Wainwright crooned. *Every kind of love, or at least my kind of love, must be an imaginary love to start with.*

"Your mom taught you how to do all this, I bet," he said after he'd pronounced the food delicious and proved it by digging in. She was proud of her rice, fluffy and perfumed with clove and cardamom.

"Some from her, yes. Mostly Tayyab. Our cook. Don't look like that!" she said when he rolled his eyes. "It's not like here. Servants...people have servants. Not just rich people. Normal people."

"I know, M'Afia. I'm just giving you a hard time." He called her that, *M'Afia*, which he said was short for *my Afia*. "What would be normal," he said, "is sharing this great meal with your brother. I bet he misses this food."

"Don't," she warned him. She held up her fork and pointed it at him.

"I'm just saying. He's my friend, too."

"He is my brother. I know him best."

He nodded. She saw his eyes go to her white knuckles, clenching her fork. "I'd like you to meet my family, anyhow," he said. "Even if I can't meet yours."

She wrinkled her brow. "You have family?"

"Sure. My mom. Sometimes my dad, I mean, they don't live together, but still."

"But—" That a mother didn't make a family was not something she could tell Gus. It would hurt his feelings to understand how many voices filled the compound in Nasirabad. "But she will not like me," she said instead. "She will think..." She set down the fork, drank her lassi. She was glad Gus didn't like beer, the way American boys did. In so many ways, he surprised her. Always wanted to know what she thought about things. When she explained about going home, in December, for her cousin's wedding, he saw nothing wrong in Maryam's being plighted to a man she had not met. He cried at sad movies. But still: his mother. "She'll think I am a bad girl."

"She'll be crazy about you."

"No, she—" She couldn't finish. A tear welled in one eye. She tucked a finger under her glasses to wipe it away. A mother would want to inspect a girl first, for her son—this, she knew, was universal, no matter what they showed on American TV. A mother would want to see how modest the girl was, how graceful. She would want to know something of the family. Such was a mother's absolute right. "I'm not ready," she managed to say.

"M'Afia. I've upset you. Come here. Come on. I'm sorry."

It was infecting her, this illness, and all she could do was open her arms wide and invite it in.

He pushed his chair back and beckoned to her. When they were alone and close like this, she almost felt at home with Gus, but in a new sense of home, home as a place where their own rules made them safe. Three weeks ago, in November, they had touched for the first time. The next week, again. Each time, he had asked permission. Would she like this? Was this all right? When he touched her, it was with both wonder and inquiry. She had seen him probing his animals, just gently enough so they did not flinch away but with enough authority to detect a bowel obstruction or a tumor. One night, studying in her dorm room, he'd swung her around in her desk chair and gently, so gently, pulled off her glasses, so the world and his face lost their outlines. Your eyes, he'd said, are the most amazing eyes in the universe. So blue. It's like you went to Saturn or somewhere and came back with those eyes. Just as gently he slid the arms of her glasses back over her ears, and his face had snapped into focus, and his lips had moved to hers.

Now she sat on his lap, and he kissed her. He stroked the mole on her cheekbone with his index finger. He took off her glasses and set them on the table. "You are a blur now," she said.

"We're all blurs," he said, and kissed her again. His voice was husky. His lips pressed on hers like little warm, moist pillows. The strange feeling started up inside her. She leaned into him and felt the hard muscles of his chest against her breasts. His mouth urged hers open. Then there was his tongue, his wet and lively tongue swimming between her teeth, and her own tongue moved and was tasting his, salty and spicy with the tikka. "Is this all right?" he asked when they pulled apart for a moment, and she meant to answer but it came out as a little groan of assent. Then their lips were together again and his hand, oh his hand, under her sweater and cupping her breast as it had needed to be cupped. Since when had it needed? She didn't know, only his fingers were warm and gentle, exploring the warm skin above and below her bra, and it was safe, they were home. "Let's lie down," he said.

"All right," she said, a little frightened but not as frightened as she knew she should be, and she couldn't pretend with him. He lifted her up, rising from the chair with her in his arms. It was only two steps over to the bed, where one of the cats hissed and sprang off as he set Afia down and lay beside her.

"You tell me, okay?" he whispered when they had kissed like that some more and his hands had found the clasp of her bra and freed it. "You tell me to stop and we'll stop." A minute later he said, "It's so good, Afia," and she felt it too, how good it was, this gradual opening to each other. She wasn't just being touched now, she was touching, the curly red hair of his chest under his T-shirt and his nipples like seeds. His jeans were stiff and hard in the middle where they pressed against hers, and she held him like that, his hips wedged into her thighs. When his lips made their way down her neck to her breasts, she heard him in her mind saying *It's so good, it's good*, because there could not be a bad thing about this loving, it wasn't possible.

She heard the slide and thump of his jeans as he pulled them off and dropped them to the floor. She raised herself onto an elbow. There was the curve of his freckled hip, the scoop of pelvic bone. So vulnerable. Softly she said, "Let me see it."

"What?"

She nodded toward his nest of hair. "Let me look at it," she said.

He lay back. She felt him trusting her. Brushing her hair back from her face, she shifted so the lamplight fell between his legs. The hair coiled there was russet, like the hair on his head. A little fat on the thighs. His penis was shorter than she had imagined, but thick, pink, curving just a little up towards his belly, the circumcised top like a smooth cap. She leaned close. He smelled like the mud floors of the village during monsoon, the sweet stink of the clay. She breathed him in. She touched her finger to the thick blue vein that ran up the inverted back of it, and Gus groaned. "M'Afia," he said. "You don't know what that does to me. I want you so much."

"You've done this," she said a little dreamily, "with other girls. Haven't you?"

"One other girl. I told you about her. Ashley, in high school. Oh, Afia, please." He took her hand and wrapped it around his penis. She felt the pulse of his blood under the thin membrane. "Let go now," he said after a few seconds. "I don't want to come, not like this."

"Come," she said. "That's screwing. Isn't it?"

"No, Afia, no. Not screwing. Not when we love each other. Here." He moved her hand away from his penis. Gently he pushed her back onto the mattress. "I love you, Afia," he said. They said that in the movies. But this wasn't the movies, this was Gus. "Let me," he said.

He moved down her body. He slid her jeans off, her underpants. He studied her belly, her mound of Venus—the hair there was too dark, too thick, she never looked at it herself, but he studied the terrain with a look of wonder in his eyes. Then he dipped his head and pressed her thighs back firmly, as if opening a pair of heavy curtains, and he put his mouth there. *There.* She felt it on her in the dirty place, and his tongue that he played in her own mouth, it played down there, finding her, pulling her out. *There.* "Please," she said, and she wanted to say that her legs mustn't be apart, this was why women back home rode motorcycles side saddle, so nothing would get between them, nothing *there.* But he muttered something, she couldn't hear, he came up for breath and then his mouth was back, deeper in the place. *There. There.* Rising, she felt herself rising. To meet him. "Please," she said again. "Please. Please. Gus. Oh, please." And her hand went to his head, his soft curls, holding him to her. *There*, and she felt herself turn inside out. She heard herself shout. Then she was weeping, she couldn't say why, and he was on her, the whole length of him, and his hips moving, his penis like a hot iron bar rubbing against her wet patch of hair. "Don't hurt me," she managed to say.

"I won't. I won't hurt you. I'd never hurt you. Oh Afia," he said. Something sticky spilled onto her belly, but she was past caring. He stopped moving. He wrapped his arms around her. He buried his face in her neck.

Some time passed. She didn't know—seconds, minutes, an hour? From above the October breeze slipped through the open windows and lapped them. "Afia, M'Afia," Gus finally said, and he gave a low chuckle.

That snapped her back. She pulled her arm out from underneath his back—it had gone to sleep a little, pinpricks below the elbow—and sat up. She felt the drying mess of his ejaculate in her pubic hair. His come. She recalled what she had done, unfolding to him like that, opening her shame, delighting in it. *Shahid*, she suddenly thought. *Shahid lala.* At the thought of her brother, of her brother's knowing what she had just done, her body contracted. She curled up like a bean sprout. Her arms wrapped her shins; her head tucked into her chest. Blindly she reached for the blanket and pulled it over her body and head. She tried not to breathe. The air hurt. It kept her shame alive.

Weakly she heard Gus talking. She felt his hand pulling at the blanket. "Honey?" he was saying. "You okay? C'mon out of there, M'Afia. Knock, knock. Come on, don't get weird on me. Honey?"

"I must go," she said into the blanket. She didn't know if he could hear her. She didn't move. "I have to go." The blanket was becoming damp with her breath. Her damn breath. Oh, to disappear.

"Here. Here, look. I'm sorry, I thought you wanted to."

Unmoving, she nodded.

"Here, let's make it better. Cover yourself with this. It'll be okay. I didn't come inside you, right? So it's not like we did anything, really. Here."

He managed to pull down the blanket so her head was out. She sneaked a look upward. He was still naked, blotchy pink, his hair disheveled the way it got when he'd played a squash match. He was holding out his bathrobe; she'd seen it hanging on a peg by the tiny bathroom built out from the far corner of the garage. It was terrycloth, navy and red plaid, frayed at the cuffs. Sitting on the edge of the bed, he managed to lift her torso as if she were an ill child. He maneuvered her arms into the sleeves. Her hair fell into her face, but she didn't brush it back—she wished it would fall heavier, become a wall between her and the world.

"Stand back," she finally managed to say. He stepped away from the bed and she rose. But once she'd knotted the belt around her waist, she didn't know what else to do. The delicious feeling that had started when he put his mouth between her legs still crept up through the center of her body, like a heavy perfume.

"Whoa," he said as she started to sway. He got his arms around her shoulders. Gently he steered her to the bathroom. His face looked so worried. She wanted him not to worry, what had happened was not his fault, but she couldn't put the words together in English. That her legs would carry her across the industrial carpet of the floor astonished her. Blurry still, without her glasses, the fish glimmered under the light of the aquarium. Rufus Wainwright wasn't singing anymore. Keeping one hand on her back, Gus reached into the rickety shower stall and turned on the spray. "You just need to wash off, Afia," he said. "Just wash me away, then you'll be okay. We love each other, okay, honey? Let me kiss you. Just once. Here."

Steam began to rise. He lifted her chin with his fingers and put his lips on hers. It was different this time, the touch like a benediction. Still she could not meet his eyes.

He untied the robe. "Go on," he said softly, slipping it from her shoulders and steering her into the stall. The water was warm and pounded her back. She stood with her hands over her breasts. Between her legs, she felt urine release. At the same time her eyes released and she began to sob. The water poured down, the tears poured, tasting of shame. Then she felt something warm and a little rough against her shoulder blades. She turned. He was in the stall with her, Gus. Naked too, and wet, he soaped up the washcloth. He ran it over her back. She had no words for him as he turned her, opened the cross of her arms so the water spilled over her front. Turned her again; knelt on the white floor of the shower. With studious care, he washed her pubic hair, her thighs. When she would not part her legs he reached around and washed between them from the back. Standing, he lifted up first one of her arms, then the other, and soaped the delicate skin underneath, the little nests of hair that she didn't shave, and turned her once more so the water would rinse off the soap. Then, quickly, he soaped and rinsed himself. When he was done, still under the steaming spray, he wrapped his arms around her, his big bearish arms. When he let her go, the water washed her again, washed away his touch. "You see?" he said, and the huskiness in his voice was gone; he sounded like a boy, a very young and hopeful boy. "It's going to be fine."

He stepped out of the shower, wrapped a towel around himself, and left her in the bathroom. After a little while, she shut off the water. The tiny room was white with steam. She groped her way out of the stall to a second clean towel that he'd left for her on the rack. She dried herself everywhere and twisted her hair up in the towel. She brushed her teeth with a finger and Gus's paste. Before she put the robe back on she touched herself, just at the top of her pubic mound. It felt softer there, like the skin of ripe fruit. When she stepped out into the room, Gus handed her back her glasses, and she slipped them on. And it all looked as it had before. This was her home in America, this was her safe place. Shahid did not know she was here; no one knew or could know. Nothing that happened here could hurt her.

Gus was standing apart from her, by Voltaire's cage. The iguana was stretching his neck up, sniffing for food. Gus's arms hung down, the palms turned toward her, waiting. Her lips parted by themselves into a smile, the pleasure making its way all the way up now and into her face. "I'm hungry," she said.

"We've got ice cream," he said.

They sat together at the rickety table, the light outside gone now, only the yellow light from the bathroom streaming across the floor. Their knees kept knocking against each other. Afia felt famished. She couldn't stop eating.

Atlantic City

HAD ALEX MEANT TO BE A BUSINESSMAN? He had not. Had not meant to carry employees, to think in any way about other carbon-based life forms except when getting laid or drunk or playing handball, all of which could be done solo but without joy. Joy in life was Alex's goal. Joy!

There they sprawled, his five main horses, in Room 1058 at the Borgata, on the double beds and in the Barcalounger by the sliding balcony doors. Three of them—Idissyou, Megabucks, and Revenge—still wore their backwards baseball caps from last night. Miamiboy, on the lounger, was sleeping. The others clicked their computer keys. The TV replayed the Cubs-Colts game from the night before. Every now and then one of the guys lifted his head and said something like "Dja see that? Fucking Randy Wells. What a douche," and one of the others lifted his head and said something about flipping the channel, but no one went for the remote. Coors, Cheez-its, and last night's pizza littered the areas of the floor that weren't already covered by track shoes and T-shirts. The odor mixed stale marijuana, Bud, and jizz. At least Alex thought it was jizz. River-17, the youngest of the bunch, a nervous kid with a stammer and thick glasses, had gone apeshit last night over the hookers at the casino. "Don't you don't you think," Alex had heard him saying to the others, one by one, as the tables ground to a finish, "don't you think we could, y'know, y'know, get get one to share?"

Alex knew they could, and said so when River-17 asked him. He nodded toward one of the older girls, whose name he didn't know but who seemed to have, like him, a troop of cadets she was bringing into the business. He didn't want his boys encountering someone too professional. He didn't want them tainted.

Alex had his own room, 1065, down the hall. Miamiboy, who'd been his first horse, had wanted to bunk in with him. Five was too many for a double room, Miamiboy had argued, and he needed his sleep if he was going to perform for Alex, and he was prepared to pay his share. But Alex had a deep craving for solitude at these mega-tournaments, and he wouldn't give up an inch of it, even for a loyal grinder like Miamiboy.

"Tables go live in an hour," Alex said now. He leaned on the headboard to get a good look at Revenge's computer screen. Revenge had three pots going on Pokerstars. He was playing aggressively, which Alex always liked. "You going to shove here?" he asked, pointing to the 6-seat Sit 'n Go at the upper right.

"I'm waiting. I want this Bluffsright guy to tank first."

"I think you should shove."

"Hold on." At the bottom table, it was Revenge's turn to bet. He had pocket 10s with a 9 and a Queen on the turn. Revenge executed a modest raise, sucking the others in.

"Good move."

"Thanks, boss."

"I still think you should shove over here."

Revenge shrugged. "It's your money," he said, and clicked the mouse. Four players folded, but the one remaining matched Revenge's all-in bet and showed Queens. "Anything else I oughta do?" Revenge asked as the program collected his chips.

"Stop listening to me," Alex said. He patted the kid's shoulder. They were all so young! Alex had celebrated his twenty-seventh birthday before coming down to Atlantic City. He'd gone with a bunch of ballers to Turning Stone, in upstate New York, and played all the casino games that poker players laughed at—roulette, blackjack, craps. He'd won four grand from a slot machine, for Chrissakes. Felicia had come along for the ride, and afterward they took a room together and the sex was very, very nice, and in the morning she said Call me when you decide to live a normal life. Her best friend Patti was pregnant already. You couldn't blame her.

But these kids. All but Miamiboy in the first year of their majority, wet behind the ears. All of them dropouts from college—and Alex hadn't pulled that stunt, oh no, he had his union card to the middle class, from a place people had heard of—and all of them broke. They didn't know they were broke yet. Idissyou, for instance, was only into Alex for $500 right now, and last month he'd taken the Sunday Mulligan for 60 grand. That meant $5200 to Alex for makeup and a split of the remainder, so Idissyou was sitting on $27,400, which could coast him for six months if he was lucky. But eventually, eventually, these donks would give up. When they started to lose, Alex would bide his time, wait for that one big cash that allowed them to clear their makeup with him. Then he would drop them.

Fagin. That was what Felicia had called him when he explained to her how the system worked with him and his horses. "In *Oliver Twist*," she said, "the guy who enslaves all the pickpockets."

"I wouldn't say *enslaves*."

"Sure. And when they get too big, he just dumps them. They have to survive on their own."

"Everyone has to survive on his own, Licia. That's the world."

"No, it isn't." She'd looked square at him, her wide jaw setting off her round hazel eyes. "The only survivors are the ones who aren't on their own. Look it up."

Alex loved Felicia. She worked for a booking agent, classical musicians. Half the time, when he was home in Boston, she had to be out late at one concert or another. She didn't mind his hours. She liked the sex, even after eighteen months. Still, she was giving him an ultimatum, and that would be the end of her. Alex felt mourning creeping up on him, like a hangover.

"C'mon." He jiggled the Barcalounger. Miamiboy scrunched up his face. "Want to scope the room."

"Fuck," said Miamiboy, which was the way he began every-thing he said. "It's a room. I bubbled the one-fifty last night. Lemme sleep."

"Yeah, you asshole. You got sucked out on. Can't believe you took that bait."

"Fuck. I'm depressed enough." Miamiboy opened his eyes. They were pale, rheumy. Miamiboy smoked too much weed. Without the weed, he would have been way smarter than Alex. "The Bitch is in the house," he said. One eyebrow went up. Miamiboy had a squashed face, like a worried squirrel. His forehead wrinkled above the lifted brow.

"No way."

"Fuck way." Miamiboy pulled the lever and shot out of the Barcalounger like a launched potato. He negotiated the floor to the bathroom, where he gargled noisily and used the toilet.

"Holy God. Holy God! Holy God!" Idissyou started shout-ing. The other two horses who were awake dropped their laptops and scurried to the bed.

"Take it down, man," hissed Megabucks, pumping his fist. "Take it down down down."

"I hate that dude." Revenge pointed to the screen. "That donkey is a douche, man. Take it."

Alex shot Miamiboy a look and headed for the door. He could see Idissyou's screen as if it floated in the air before him. Final table of a 72-man Hold'em tourney, 26-grand payout to the winner. Idissyou might take fourth for 9K. That would make a good day for Idissyou, and he'd hand more than half over to Alex. It behooved Alex to act like this was no news at all, like he expected final tables from his horses even though Idissyou was the first to cash in four days and the buy-ins for that period mounted to more than $50,000 by now for the four of them, not counting Miamiboy. Excitement meant empathy and led to pity, and next thing you knew you were loaning the horse his September rent.

Outside blazed. This East Coast light! Alex slipped on his

shades and went the long way around, by the boardwalk. Not a businessman, but a vagabond with deep stashes of cash—that had been his vision. Pick up and go wherever. Breathe the air of strange mountains, rush like blood through the arteries of new cities.

"Fuck, man. Hold up." Miamiboy was getting a pretzel with mustard from the stand at the gate. His real name was Mike, and he wasn't from Miami—he was from St. Louis, like Alex— but Alex never thought of him that way anymore. He'd picked Miamiboy as his handle after they took the bus down there spring break of Mike's freshman year and Alex's junior year, and Mike had never gone back. He probably thought of Alex the same way—not as Alex anymore, but as Assassinato, which Alex had picked when both *Badass* and *Assbad* proved taken. Sometimes Alex thought of himself as Assassinato, though not recently. His online persona had hit a long dry spell. Hope lay, now, in the live game.

"You seen the schedule?" he asked Miamiboy. The kid shook his head, his mouth full of baked dough. "You're at Table Five," he said, "which I think is way down by the doors to the kitchen. They got me at Table Thirty."

"Fuck, you don't sound happy about it."

"Mike Mahoney's in Seat Two. That can't make anyone happy. And that other guy, the Swedish guy who took down Turning Stone?"

"Unpronounceable Nameson Nameson."

"Yeah, that guy. Looks like he killed three grandmothers yesterday. And he's next to me."

"Horses?"

"Idissyou's at my table. No one we know at yours."

They meandered through the casino, by the emphysemic women at the slots and the pork-bellied rounders at the craps tables. Alex kept his eyes away from the dealeresses, which was what he and Loseflips, his mentor back in the day, had called the girls in the suits. He just found them so sexy, with their tight men's jackets and that stern makeup. Ballbusters, every one of them. Once—despite Loseflips's advice—he'd asked one out, in Germany. She'd been going off her shift, so she had the jacket off. She'd smashed his face against her crisp white blouse—he would forever remember the gardenia of her breasts—then pushed him away and laughed.

He managed not to look, and then they were showing their I.D.'s to the eggplant-skinned guy by the back door, and then they were in. "They smell the same," he said to Miamiboy.

"Who do?"

"All these places."

"Fuck, they look the same. They are the same."

You couldn't name the smell. Cheap carpet cleaner and vomit maybe, but no one vomited in these rooms. Sweat, maybe. Nothing could stop it in here, and the stink escaped the armpits and settled into the carpet, the felt on the tables, the yellow chandeliers. Bacteria, Alex thought.

"Assassinato, man. Long time." He turned to see Bich Nguyen—known, of course, as the Bitch, but Bich was the guy's real name for fuck's sake, and not pronounced the same at all—mincing over the red carpet. Bich was Vietnamese. He weighed maybe a hundred pounds. Nicest guy on the poker planet, people always said of him. But Alex knew Bich had connections, not pretty ones.

"Bit," said Alex, pronouncing it the right way. "Congrats on that Florida win."

"Lucky cards," said Bich. He flashed small white teeth. "Got your ponies with you?"

"This here's my main stallion," Alex said, nodding toward Miamiboy. "The others are coming, yeah."

"Good, good." Bich reached a manicured hand out to Miamiboy, who took it and winced at the grip. "Saw you bubble the Sunday Mulligan. Tough beat."

"Fucking Queens," Miamiboy said, meaning the hand the other guy had held, but Alex saw Bich wince a little. "I admire your game, man. Look forward to railing you here."

"Yeah, well." Bich looked around the room, as if expecting the objects in it to lift and float. "This is just play, you know. Child's play."

"Zat right?" Alex folded his arms. "So where's the real business, Confucius?"

Bich smirked. He turned to Alex. Alex gave Miamiboy a little nod, and the stallion loped off to check the place cards at the tables.

"You got two horses at a soft table," Bich said when Miamiboy was out of earshot. "You know there's stakes on them."

"On my guys?" Alex reached under his baseball cap to scratch his head. He couldn't say he knew Bich. He was one of the Asians, like Alex was one of the Americans. And okay, shoot him for incorrectness, but the Asians were inscrutable. The Italians were verbose. The Americans were fat. "Who's betting on my guys?"

"Not for final table. Small stakes. Incremental." Bich's accent came out only on the tricky words. *Inclemental*. Alex thought of bad weather.

"Does that mean you've got bets in on final table? On me?" Alex fought a knot of self-consciousness. Years in this business, and the things he didn't know.

"We're not talking final table. But listen up. We need you to throw one of them."

"We? Who's we?"

"Odds are weaker on River-seven."

"Seventeen," Alex corrected him. "River-seventeen."

"And the other one"—Bich checked a scrap of paper from his beast pocket—"Leevenge."

"Revenge."

"Got some multi-accounting issues online. Too bad." Bich clucked his tongue.

"Well, I'm not instructing one of my guys to take a dive to please some bookie out there. If that's what you're suggesting."

51

"Multi-accounting," Bich went on, as if Alex hadn't spoken. "Could get nasty."

"Assass." Miamiboy had trotted back from the tables. "Fuck, I just saw the Swedish dude. He is so coked up. You can *take* him here, man. He's about to start bleeding through his pores."

"What've you got to do with online?" Alex asked Bich. He ignored Miamiboy. Bich was nodding, his chin doing little quick dips, like he was overseeing work that he approved of. "What've you got to do with anyone's play online?"

Delicately Bich pulled a miniature leather folder from his back pocket, and with his slim yellowish fingers he extracted a business card. *B.R.W. Nguyen*, it read. *Advissory Committee, PokerStars*. Gold lettering on a red and black background. Trust the Asians to rule the world without ever figuring out double consonants. By the time Alex looked up from proofreading the card, Bich was gone.

•

He commissioned Miamiboy to run back and get the guys out and down to the tables. Half-hour left. He stepped out of the casino, past the uniformed bellhops and the line of cabs chuffing patiently by the curb. He needed to think. He didn't like what Bich was saying. He didn't like being blindsided. And then there were the bonds of affection. "Yes, dammit," he heard himself whispering as he cut from the parking lot to the manicured lawn and path around the lake and fountain, "they *are* bonds of affection. Bitch," he added, talking not to Bich Nguyen but to Felicia, in his head. He *knew* Revenge. He'd got Revenge's weed habit down to three joints a day. He'd heard the kid on the phone to his mom—his mom who had breast cancer, for fuck's sake—and the kid was all choked up. Last year he and Revenge took out Jet Skis in Aruba, and Revenge couldn't find the decelerator when they were bringing them in, and he crashed into the dock. Broke his collarbone, but he never bawled about that. So maybe the kid was multi-accounting. What business was that of Bich Nguyen's?

He'd made his way down to the lake. Man-made for sure, a perfect oval. The bushes stood trimmed, the grass like a nubby carpet. In the calmer water, away from the lofted spray, calico carp undulated. Only on the far side did goose droppings mar the scene. He used to feed the geese, on the scrubby pond in Massachusetts where they spent summers after his mom married Tim the Toaster Man. They called him that because on the second date, the guy brought over a new toaster for the family. He sold appliances and had the slick look to go with the job, the trim mustache and the wheedling voice. But when he caught Alex feeding the geese, Tim collared him. You feed rats, too? Tim asked, and next morning he got out his 20-gauge and blew away six of the adults, leaving the goslings to *cheep* disconsolately on the bloody grass until the heron took two and the cats got the rest.

Shut up, stupid, he told himself. He wasn't feeding geese now. He was in the black with his stable, not by much, but he could feel the horses learning discipline, channeling their talent. Now he had to throw one of them under the bus or Bich Nguyen would out Revenge for multi-accounting. And who else was doing it? Miamiboy, Megabucks? He remembered the drinks Megabucks had put down the night they arrived, the table dancer he tipped with a hundred. The guy was supposed to be into Alex for eight grand, but for all Alex knew he was playing against himself with some other backer and was up six figures. Trust. What a rare commodity.

Returning, he stopped at the bar for an energy drink, kombucha with a shot of blackberry. The guys at the bar were older, balding, stinking of cologne and cigars. "Fuck, they were never us," Miamiboy said, sidling up to him, nodding at the regulars. "And we'll never be them."

"Keep telling yourself," said Alex.

"The ponies are coming down," said Miamiboy.

"Good. I need to talk to Revenge."

"Except the River."

Alex turned to him. Miamiboy had donned his shades already, getting prepared for the table. They made him look like a fly. "He's not still online, is he? What a donk."

"Fuck no. He's disappeared, man. Nobody saw him slip out."

"So maybe he's on the floor already."

"Fuck, I checked his table."

"Stay here, buddy." Alex downed the kombucha, wiping his mouth with the back of his hand. The lobby was a sea of baseball caps and hoodies, with sexpot broadcasters for the internet squeezing out airpockets to interview one rising hopeful or another. He pushed his way past, down the corridor, through the oval entrance to the poker room. It was filling now, guys thrumming their knees under the tables. The chandeliers hung down like spiders. The walls glowed gold. His own table was in Bobby's Room, where they usually put the high stakes, but it meant nothing now—every foot of floor space was taken up with a felt-topped table and high-backed chairs. The railers would have to squeeze against the curved walls. He found Revenge at Table Twelve, texting. "Man, where's River?"

"Who gives a fuck? Guy's a douche. You should never of let him in the stable."

Irritation climbed up from Alex's gut. "Don't talk like that. Tough to be at the same table, but so what? Seven other guys can lose."

"Assass, you should of seen him last night. With women? Seriously."

"I don't want to hear it. We've got to find him."

"Why?"

"So he can go down, asshole. So you don't have to. And then we talk."

He saw Revenge's eyes flick over to the corner—where, sure enough, Bich Nguyen stood still as a museum guard. If River-17 didn't show, the bets were off. And if the Bitch busted Revenge, the scandal would taint all of Assassinato's stable. Who'd back him then? Either he was into it himself or he was a tool. He pushed out of the room and clawed his way to the elevators.

Joy. That was the endgame, he thought as the glass cube rose heavenward. That was the final pot. Loseflips, when he quit, had these gray circles under his eyes, and the eyes themselves had shrunk back in his head as if they couldn't handle too much light. He'd moved to Costa Rica. Alex visited once. There were girls everywhere, and a dwarf making Mai Tais at the bar by the swimming pool, but it was still depressing. Loseflips went around in Hawaiian-print jams, his chest and belly leathery and sagging. He painted big, garish oils of the sunset. He was content, Loseflips said. Pleasure filled his life. Note: *not joy.* That was three years ago; plenty of invitations since. Alex wasn't going back.

He used his key to get into the horses' room. The maids had done their best, stacked the sweaty clothes onto the chairs, tucked the game gear into the video cabinet, tossed out the containers, made the beds. "River?" he said. No answer. He checked his watch. Twelve minutes to show time. If River didn't show, Revenge would have to go down. Multi-accounting thief, anyhow. Problem was he liked Revenge. Never grow fond of your horses, Loseflips had told him, you run a stable not a nursery. He called Miamiboy on the cell. "Any sign?"

"Idissyou said he was in the room."

"Tell Revenge to take a fall. Not in the first hand. Maybe five hands in."

"Fuck, Assass. Is it the accounting? Because I can tell you—"

"Don't tell me. Tell Revenge. I don't have time."

"You fucking owe me for this."

"Miami." He was out in the hallway now, clicking the door shut behind him. "It is not possible for me to owe you."

Nine minutes. He'd do a line. He'd promised Felicia to stop, but Felicia didn't understand the pressure of being a businessman. Pulling out his own room card, he sidled down the hall and slipped it into the lock of 1065. There, in the bright light streaming through the filmy white curtains, he saw the skinny, drooping ass of River-17, above River-17's skinny hairy thighs, thrusting up against a big stuffed panda bear, the kind you get at the state fair. "Oof," River-17 was saying.

"Ungh," said the panda bear. Only Alex realized it wasn't a panda bear. It was a maid, a fat maid with her face smashed into the plaid coverlet and her black dress hiked over her wide hips.

"What the hell," Alex said, and the panda maid turned her face, and he saw she wasn't just fat but old. Middle-aged, anyhow. The legs were streaked with varicosities. The face— Latina, that almond look to the eyes—was brick-colored with exertion, pocked and wrinkled. Her little black-and-white hat fell askew.

"*Perdoname*," she said, and in less than a second she was out from under River-17, standing chunky on the carpet, pulling up her brown stockings. She'd kept her shoes on, squat black leather with fat heels. "*Perdon, perdon.*"

River-17 staggered back from the bed. His penis stuck out from him like a pointing finger. "K-K-K-Christ, what time is it?"

"Too late for you, asshole."

"Look, I can, I can explain. The guys were all in the room, right? And last night—I didn't manage it last night, and I knew I couldn't concentrate if—if—"

"My room," said Alex. "This is my fucking room."

"I know, and it's, it's really bad, and if I hadn't—last night—"

Alex looked at his watch again. "You got seven minutes to be at the table. We'll settle later."

The maid was on her knees, now, fumbling for Alex's hand, whispering *perdon, perdoname*. A bruise, on her cheekbone. Jesus, he thought. Compassion blazed through him. He lifted her up. "I'm sorry," he said. He pulled a twenty from his billfold and pushed it into her hand. "Let the room be, it's fine."

He counted to ten after she left. He checked the hallway.

Empty. River was hopping on one leg, struggling into his pants. He looked like a marionette, all out of joint. Alex threw the rest of his clothes into the hall. "Move," he said, shoving the kid.

He shut the door after him.

Five minutes to show time. He wouldn't do the line. It wouldn't make a difference now. He was too far down. In the bathroom, he splashed cold water onto his face. He tried to shake off the image, the sounds, River-17 with his noodly member raping the hotel help. The awful thing was that the scene he'd just witnessed was making his own dick rise in his pants. He wanted the maid. He wanted her more than the dealeresses, more than Felicia. He wanted everything about her. Her generous hips, her heavy bruised cheek. He wanted to find her wherever she'd gone—to the linen closet, in with the starched sheets—and thrust his sympathy on her.

But that wasn't joy. Was it? His mission—he smirked at himself, making even this a duty—was to seek joy. Exiting the room, Alex was relieved to find the hall empty. Nothing had happened. His horses rumbled downstairs, calling to him, kicking up dust with their heels, their eyes on the cliff edge ahead, the blue sky after.

Luxembourg

SPYING THE GI AT THE LUGGAGE CAROUSEL in Frankfurt, Melissa thought first of her brother Ned. Ned was in Vietnam, drafted. Melissa worried about him all the time. She had fallen in love in order to stop worrying over Ned. Now love had brought her to Europe, away from the protests and the TV reports, and here was the GI, reminding her.

He must be on his way to Vietnam, she thought. Guilt put a sour taste into her mouth. Then she remembered that American forces were still in Germany. They were left over from World War II, her dad's war. Suddenly the GI looked soft and surly in his fatigues, a volunteer who played baseball in Europe while Ned sweated in the jungle. She averted her eyes. Too late.

"Where you headed?" the GI asked, sidling up to Melissa. He had a pimple on the side of his nostril, green eyes, a scar on his square chin.

"Luxembourg," she said, clipping the word. "For a program," she added. She wasn't going to let him tease her about bumming around Europe. Melissa had never been to Europe before, and wasn't all that curious about the place. Across the carousel, three skinny travelers leaned their heads together, lighting up cigarettes. The two girls had boob-length straight hair, one tied back with a pale bandanna, the other with a leather circlet around her forehead. The guy was tall, with wire-rims and a long, hooked nose; his vest had a peace sign embroidered on the back. Melissa felt the GI's eyes flick over to the hippies and back to her.

"Well, whaddayaknow," he said. He shifted a toothpick from one side of his mouth to the other. "I'm heading to Luxembourg myself. I can give you a lift."

"That's okay," she said. The GI had the bullet-shaped head of all shorn soldiers, the thick neck that would have made Ned's neck look frail as a flower stem. "I've got the train schedule. But thank you," she said, trying to make gratitude a dismissal. Ned had warned her about assholes in the military.

"No, look. Look," the GI said. He touched her elbow lightly. He pointed to the end of the carousel, where a family stood waiting for their bags. "I'm taking them," he said, "to the American base in Luxembourg. That's what I'm here to do. We go right by the center of the city. I can take you anywhere you want."

He had a broad twang; Texas, or Oklahoma. Melissa was from Ohio, taking a break from school in Michigan. She pictured a broad swath down the middle of the country, the way Frankfurt sat in the middle of Europe. She and this GI were both from places you could leave to go somewhere, anywhere. Reluctantly, she regarded the family. The mom stood behind her two kids, a sleepy-looking girl and a chunky boy whose hair stood up in tufts. Next to her, the dad checked his watch. They were all the ages of the families Melissa had babysat for in high school. "You're taking them?" she said, not looking at the GI. "Isn't your car full?"

"I've got the Air Force van."

"And you'd deposit me first. At the train station there."

"Wherever you like. Come on, kid. You'll meet them. You'll see." He had her elbow, now, and was steering her. As they wove through the patient crowd, he stuck out his hand. "I'm Charlie," he said.

"Melissa." She found herself taking the hand. She tried to smile. Quickly she did the arithmetic in her head. The train was sixty Deutschmarks, fifteen bucks. She had only two hundred in traveler's checks. And if Charlie was taking a family...

The mom eyed Melissa up and down and said, "We've got a lot of luggage."

"I'll take the train," Melissa said quickly.

"No, no," said Charlie. He addressed himself to the dad.

"We've got plenty of space in the back," he said, "and a rack on top. Young lady needs a lift."

"I do not—" Melissa began.

The dad winked at Charlie. His free hand went to his wife's neck and gave it a quick squeeze. "We'll be fine," he said. He introduced himself as Lawrence McGilroy. Betsy was his wife. Melissa didn't catch the kids' names. They were there, Mr. McGilroy explained, to set up a new personnel office on the Air Force base just inside the German border from Luxembourg. They were expanding the plant, making it permanent. The McGilroys expected to be in Luxembourg for three years. Betsy McGilroy did not look happy about the arrangement. The luggage had started to float down the stream of the carousel. Melissa felt trapped by the family, the GI, her own desire to save a little cash. She looked over at the hippies. They would take this ride, she told herself. They wouldn't hesitate.

What brought Melissa to Europe? Mr. McGilroy wanted to know while they waited for Charlie to pull the van around. He stood between Melissa and the rest of his family. Melissa didn't want to talk to him. She wanted to talk to Betsy, to explain that she was not some easy girl who got herself picked up at luggage carousels. Instead she found herself telling Mr. McGilroy everything she had told her parents—that she was taking a break from college, that she had found an organization that would arrange a job for her in Austria, that she wanted to experience working life before she settled on a major.

None of this perfectly reasonable explanation touched the truth. Melissa had come to Europe out of determined and passionate love. Nothing short of death or despair would keep her from her quest.

Mr. McGilroy nodded and stroked his day-old beard. Why shouldn't he believe Melissa? She was a dumpling of a young woman, russet-haired and heavy in the hips, with a round face and a strong jaw. All her life, people's expectations had been that she would plug away, hang on to her female friends, satisfy herself with a just portion—or slightly less—of life's rewards. Even Ned, who spoiled her, described her to his friends as a good egg.

Three months ago, right after she got the letter from Ned saying he was headed for Nam, Melissa had distracted herself by going to a frat party. She had found herself on an oversized pillow next to an anthro major named Dave. They had gone through the list of people they knew in common, and when they hit on the name "Elliot Groverman," Dave's pot-dilated eyes had widened further. "Wait," he had said—giving the word two syllables, *way-et*. "Aren't you the Melissa Elliot's in love with?"

Up to that moment, Melissa had not given Elliot Groverman a second thought. He was an art major who wore pants splattered with paint. He'd sat next to her in a class on Nietzsche. One day he had asked her to cut his hair. She had borrowed sharp scissors from a friend who worked in the theater's costume department, met Elliot on the quad, and snipped his dark, curly locks to a length just below his small ears. She had assumed he had asked her because she looked competent. He was usually surrounded by females. She stared at Dave and frowned. "Don't put me on," she said.

"I am not kidding you, man. The guy was getting on the plane for Vienna, for his year abroad thing, and he said, 'You know, I think I am in love with Melissa.' I told him it was a tough life, dude, and he got on the plane."

Melissa was not a virgin. She had enjoyed a practical though clumsy relationship last year with another freshman whom her best friend, Anna, had turned down, and she might have been sleeping with him still had he not kept pinching her nipples. She had a diaphragm tucked into her suitcase. She didn't like the Pill. It made you fat and cranky, everyone said. She had accepted that she would make a life out of the materials she could scrape together. She would never be the sort of woman with whom any but the psychically disturbed would fall madly in love. Elliot Groverman was not psychically disturbed, so either Dave had misheard him, or Melissa was wrong about her fate. *Amor fati*, that was what Nietzsche had written. She had jotted it in her notebook in that class, sitting next to Elliot Groverman. *Amor fati*, love your fate.

Thus far, Melissa had carried out her plan with the veneer of reasonableness for which she was known. She had counted up her college credits and discovered that she would need only one summer course to stay on track. She had determined— through idle chat, through careful listening—that Elliot was taking a semester of courses at the university in Vienna and then planning to travel around Europe. She had researched and discovered this program—SOS, for Student Overseas Services—that placed American students in temporary jobs. She had picked up the text for first-year German and studied on her own. From Elliot's friend Dave—again idly, and only after the other arrangements were in place—she had obtained Elliot's address. She had dropped him a carefully chosen art postcard with a few throwaway lines about how she would coincidentally be in the same country as he, and how she might want to travel. *Amor fati*, she had written at the bottom, and then she had scratched it out and bought another card and written the same thing but without the line from Nietzsche. Finally, she had done the unforgivable. She had informed her parents that worry over Ned, over Ned's safety and Ned's well-being, were keeping her from focusing on her studies, and she had to go out in the world and do her small part to show the world that not all Americans were pigs.

"Isn't it usually the junior year for going abroad?" her mother had asked. And her father had added, "Why don't you *study* something, over there?"

But Melissa had heaved large sighs when she was home over Thanksgiving. To confirm her disenchantment with school, she had deliberately pulled a C in Shakespeare.

Now here she was, in the center of Europe. Every bit of her

plan had worked so far. Even the postcard she had received back from Elliot Groverman, with its crabbed script and the suggestion that she write again when she was on "this side of the pond," gave her hope. Luxembourg was the headquarters of SOS. She had a three-day orientation there before receiving her papers and a train ticket to the ski hotel in Austria where she was to work. Eventually Elliot would find her. He would be madly in love with her. Her life, the predictable course of her life, would erupt. "That," she remembered Ned saying about getting his draft notice, "was when my life began to change." His change was war. Melissa's would be love.

The van pulled up to the curb. Charlie lifted all the bags into the back and got the family installed. How Melissa ended in the middle of the wide front seat, with Charlie at the wheel on her left and the stocky boy kicking his feet on her right, she could not say. She had not slept on the plane. It was mid-morning in Germany, but she felt lost in both space and time.

"You folks hungry?" Charlie asked as they pulled away from the airport. It was drizzling slightly, the control towers fogged in. All the road signs were in German. The cars were mostly tiny, with rounded edges.

"Could eat a horse," said Mr. McGilroy.

"We need to get to the house," his wife said.

"Do they have hamburgers?" said the daughter from the back seat.

They did, as it turned out. Melissa wrinkled her nose at the place Charlie took them to, a small Army base an hour away. "Air Force base is much bigger," he explained as they settled with their cafeteria trays at a Formica table that might have been a rest stop on any American highway. "We got three hundred families living on base now, plus four thousand enlisted guys, and then of course the executives like you who rent off base. We got a school for you kids"—he mussed the boy's hair—"and a church, a swimming pool. You'll see. Just like home."

Melissa looked at the gray patty on her plate, the spongy

bun. Ned's letters were full of complaint about this sort of thing—the American bases in Vietnam, a damp country full of mountains and fog, that were tricked out like a prefab version of Kansas. "Anybody speak German?" she asked.

"On base?" Charlie snorted. The children, confused, laughed as if Melissa had made a joke.

"It's all English now," said Betsy McGilroy.

"Ah, but the fraüleins," said Mr. McGilroy. He winked at Charlie, who had lit a cigarette and blew smoke toward the ceiling.

"Don't need too many words there," Charlie said. "Hey, Melissa?"

"I'm going to be working," she said—realizing, suddenly, that no one had asked why she had chosen Europe, what her plan was—"as a waitress. In Austria. I'll be speaking German all day."

"Well, I'll be," said Mr. McGilroy. "Good for you, honey."

Betsy McGilroy put her arm around her daughter and drew her close, as if the atmosphere around them had grown dangerous.

Talk turned to the war in Vietnam, the terrible politics Stateside. How could Melissa have thought she could get away from it? Nixon had just announced a new bombing campaign. "But he's bringing the boys home," Mr. McGilroy said. "That's what those acid heads in California don't understand. You can't just yank your troops out and abandon the people you're fighting for."

"You marching against the war, Melissa?" Charlie asked. Mr. McGilroy chuckled; his wife rolled her eyes.

Melissa thought about Ned. But Ned wouldn't like these people, and she didn't want to expose him to them. "I don't know what we're doing over there," she said, "if that's what you're asking."

"Oh, I'm not asking that, honey." Mr. McGilroy winked again at Charlie. He had a tic, Melissa decided, a winking tic. "I know better than to ask a question like that. You see, I know

I am not an expert on the Communist threat."

"Unlike some people," said his wife.

Melissa concentrated on her lemonade. She reminded herself she had a goal. She would not be derailed. Ned, she thought incongruously. Ned, stay with me here.

After the meal, while the rest of them visited the restroom, Charlie swung the van around. "Y'all just catch forty winks now," he said as they filed into the car. "Three hours to Luxembourg."

"Train station first," Melissa reminded him. They were all taking their same places. She was the hitchhiker; she had no right to ask for a different seat.

"You got it, fraülein," Charlie said.

They roared onto the Autobahn. Within seconds, it seemed, Melissa fell asleep. When she woke up, they were leaving the highway, bumping onto a secondary road. Charlie's arm lay around her shoulders. His right hand gripped her breast. She jerked upright. He gave the flesh a squeeze, then released it. He said nothing. Melissa twisted around. They were all asleep— the boy with his head wedged between the back of the seat and the door, Betsy McGilroy drooling onto her husband's shoulder, Mr. McGilroy with his head thrown back. Only the blond daughter eyed her. The little girl's blue eyes stared accusingly at Melissa; she pinched her rosebud lips together. Melissa cleared her throat.

"How much longer?" she said, just loud enough to wake anyone who might be simply dozing.

"Not long," said Charlie, but he kept his voice low. His hand strayed to Melissa's knee, which she pulled away. "What're you really doing here, anyhow," he said.

"I told you. I've got a job. My boyfriend"—she licked her lips, which felt dry and cracked—"is studying art in Vienna. So it's a way for us to be together."

"College boy, huh," said Charlie. He checked the rear view mirror, then executed a sharp left turn. They began climbing.

High brick walls, the walls of a suburb, bordered the road, with glimpses of roofs on the other side. On the narrow sidewalk, Luxembourgers waited patiently for the bus. They wore snug wool coats and scarves and chunky-heeled leather shoes. They waited for buses differently from people in America. She was in a foreign country, Melissa suddenly realized. Of ordinary lives here, lives like hers, she understood nothing.

"Elliot's a friend of my brother's," Melissa lied smoothly. "My brother's in Vietnam."

"Drafted, I guess," said Charlie.

Melissa considered protesting this. He made it sound like getting drafted was a wussy thing to do. She hated this guy. She hated the idea that he'd been fondling her breast while she slept. She hated his shorn head and bull neck, she hated how he jollied this family along. She wanted to put the fact of Elliot in front of him, of Elliot's art and Elliot's love for her. But as she blinked her eyes and sat up, for the first time in weeks she could not even bring an image of Elliot Groverman to mind. Had he ever said he loved her? He must have been joking, or day-dreaming. He must have had the wrong name. There must have been another Melissa. He had never approached her except to cut his hair. He had never called her; had sent no postcard from Vienna until she wrote to say that by happenstance she would be in the area. She had invented this idea of a dormant passion that she would journey to Europe and awaken. She was a good egg, Ned had said. She was not a girl with whom artists fell madly in love. And now she was bumping along in this van next to a GI who smelled of ketchup and cigarettes and something sour.

In the back, Betsy McGilroy stirred. "My goodness," she said. "I slept."

"Almost there, Ma'am," Charlie said. He grinned at her through the rear view. They had risen past the walled slopes to more open sprawl, almost like an American suburb. He turned right into a new development. Mr. McGilroy shook himself awake. The little girl, still staring, kicked at the back of Melissa's seat. Charlie pulled to a stop in the driveway of a gambrel-roofed house.

"But—" Melissa began.

He grinned at her. The muscles in his neck worked as if he were chewing and swallowing. "Easier to drop these folks off first," he said. "They've got a lot to sort out. Don't you, sir?"

"Damn straight," said Mr. McGilroy. He stepped out of the van and stretched. The door to the house opened, and a small woman stood in it, waving.

"Who's *that*?" said the girl loudly.

"I think her name's Louise," said Charlie, sliding out of the van. "Colonel sent her over, to help you folks get unpacked."

On Melissa's right, the boy still slept soundly, his mouth open, a pearl of saliva hanging from his lower lip. She scooted left and out the driver's door. She looked around. In every direction stood new houses, with spindly trees in the yards. She had no idea where the city of Luxembourg lay. Her suitcase in the back of the van was packed for six months, three of them winter in the Alps. As she started toward the house, Charlie tried to catch her arm. She shook him off.

Betsy was in the house already. The front door hung open. Inside, boxes stood in every room, along with furniture draped in plastic. Louise, who was a sharp-nosed blonde not much older than Melissa, was listening as Betsy made her way through the rooms, saying they would have to move this or that, and where was Lawrence's desk, and she'd thought there were two full baths.

"*Bitte*," Melissa said to Louise in her best German. "*Wo is die Bahnhof?*"

Louisa knit her transparent brows. "Excuse me?"

"*Die Bahnhof?* Train station? *Ich bin…*" Melissa searched for the word for *lost*. "*Ich muss an Bahnhof gehen.*"

"I speak only French," Louise said. "And English," she added. Betsy McGilroy was back, having descended another staircase. Melissa followed her into the kitchen. "Please, Mrs. McGilroy," she said. Adults had always liked her. She reminded herself how many times she had babysat for couples like the McGilroys. "I know what you've been thinking," she said as quickly as possible. "But I wouldn't have taken this ride. I was going to take the train. Except that Charlie pointed you out. I mean, he pointed out that he was taking a family. So I felt safe. But I don't feel safe now. He promised me he would leave me at the train station before he brought you here. I don't want to be alone with him."

All this came out very fast, in a breathy voice that even to Melissa didn't sound very convincing. "I don't know what you expect me to do," Betsy McGilroy said.

"I don't know. Maybe…maybe your husband could come along. Just down to the train station. Or we could call a cab."

"How do you do that, in this country?" Betsy McGilroy asked.

Her daughter was tugging on her arm. She went back upstairs. In the front foyer, Charlie was setting down pairs of valises. Melissa turned back to Louise. But the housekeeper, or whatever she was, looked Melissa up and down and then retreated to the kitchen, her heels clacking. Finally, as Charlie brought the last pair of bags, Melissa saw the McGilroys on the landing of the front stairs. Betsy was speaking to her husband with what looked like urgency. Mr. McGilroy scratched the back of his head. Reluctantly, he nodded.

"That's it," said Charlie. "I'll let you folks settle in. Base commander'll be by tomorrow, get your schedule set up. Meanwhile, if you need anything, you can ask Louise." With his hand, he beckoned Melissa. "Let's get going."

"Say," said Mr. McGilroy. He descended the steps heavily. He did not look at Melissa. "I'm curious to see a little of the town. Mind if I come along?"

Charlie grinned. "Not at all," he said.

Melissa sighed with relief. They made their way down the

stone walk to the van. She started for the back seat, but Mr. McGilroy held the passenger door open and welcomed her in. Well, that was all right; it was a wide seat. Charlie had already started the engine. As she pulled the door shut, he leaned across her to where Mr. McGilroy was opening the back door. "Listen," Charlie said. "You get settled with your family. I'll come back in the morning, give you a grand tour."

"Well, I don't know," Mr. McGilroy began. His gaze skittered around the interior of the van, anywhere but on Melissa's face.

"You and the missus, if you like. Louise can handle the kids."

"I am a little tired," Mr. McGilroy said. He stepped away from the car. He winked, whether at Melissa or Charlie it was impossible to say.

No, Melissa whispered.

But already Charlie was backing out of the drive, turning, waving to Mr. McGilroy where he stood on the stone path. Betsy McGilroy stood in the doorway, watching them leave.

As they descended the long slope, Charlie said nothing. At the bottom of the hill they stopped at a red light. Melissa considered jumping out. But there was her suitcase, in the far back. Charlie hung a left, a different direction from the one they had come. They rumbled along a cobbled street, with houses tight together, tiny gardens in the front now burlapped for winter. From a few blocks' distance Melissa heard a siren, the sort she had heard only in movies about World War II, those lower and upper tones like a seesaw. The van swung around a small roundabout, then another. They were leaving the houses behind.

"Train station," she said after the second roundabout. "Remember? Train station?"

"You don't have a brother in Vietnam," Charlie said. He kept his eyes on the road. His mouth pulled to one side.

"I do too! He's in Danang. Better than—" but she cut herself off. He was baiting her.

"You got no boyfriend either. You made that up."

69

"Will you just take me to the train station?"

"You're too plug ugly for a boyfriend. You came to Europe to get yourself a little free love, didn't you?"

Melissa didn't answer this. They had entered a wood, an endless row of beeches leaning across the road. She tightened her grip on the leather strap of her shoulder bag. When Charlie pulled the van over to the side of the road and lunged for her, she hit him with it on his bullet head.

The blow broke his pimple. His green eyes widened.

"Whoah ho," he said, his voice husky. "Little hostile there, aren'tcha?"

"You said you'd take me to the station! Before you let them off!"

"You never believed that." He was moving closer to her on the seat. She made to hit him again with the pocketbook, but he grabbed her wrist. "You jumped into this car like a fish into a pond."

She could smell him, he was so close. He smelled like Ned when he was home on leave, before he got shipped over. Sour and tinged with chlorine. It must be the military soap, she thought. Then he put his mouth on hers, pushing her back against the doorframe. He was going to rape her. He was going to rape her because she'd lied about Elliot. Because she was an idiot. Her hand still gripping the shoulder strap, Melissa managed to pull the latch on the car door. When it opened, she fell onto the hard road. She hit her back on a stone. The breath flew out of her. Gasping, she struggled to her feet.

Charlie was leaning out the door, one leg crooked underneath him on the seat. His eyes looked like flat coins. He laughed. "Where you going, little girl?"

"You take me to the train station," Melissa said, "or I will walk."

He rubbed his chin. He seemed to consider this. Then he exited by the driver's door, went around to the back of the van, and pulled out her suitcase. He set it in the road. He stepped toward her.

"I'll hurt you," said Melissa. She gripped the strap of the pocketbook. Her lips trembled. She wanted to cry.

He snorted. "You're not worth fucking," he said. He got back into the van, threw it into reverse, and ran over Melissa's suitcase. She heard the frame crunch under the wheels. She put a fist to her mouth. The van spun around and moved off, dust in its wake.

For a minute, Melissa panted. Then she made herself stop. It was eerie, to be so suddenly alone. She lifted the handle of the ruined suitcase and dragged it to the side of the road. The train station had to be back the way they came. Four miles? Five? They didn't even have miles here. Kilometers. Trees rose on both sides of the road, their bare branches glistening with the morning's sleet. No houses as far as she could see. Her shoulder blade hurt where she'd hit the road. She sat on the crushed lid of the suitcase. For the second time that afternoon, she tried to think of Elliot Groverman and couldn't. She had no longer come here for Elliot, or for love. She had come here to be alone in this gray wood, in this old country, and to make her way out. Charlie's face, when she whacked him with the pocketbook, had filled with a dumb rage that set her free from all her plans, all her silly dreams.

She would tell Ned the story, when she saw him. She would say, "That's when my life began to change." Out of the fog a car appeared, not the van but a Luxembourgian car, rounded and small. Melissa rose and put out her thumb.

The House of My Other Life

THE BLACKBERRY BRANDY'S ALL DONE. I tip the pint upward—
not even a dark droplet rolls out—and set it back on the tea
table I've unfolded by my much-abused bed. Time to haul
my ass out from under the covers. Stand. When the dizziness
passes, I adjust my sanitary pad like a boxer fixing his jock strap
and get to work on the plaster.

A half-dozen boxes of dried plaster sit on the floor of my
studio apartment. The kid, Jorge, knocked it all down from
the wall dividing the place in two, and he probably hauled out
a dozen boxes' worth himself before I paid him and let him
go. I couldn't afford him anymore. Plus, I had to recover from
this abortion I had two days ago, which hit me a lot harder
than I thought it would—they tell you it's like period cramps,
don't believe a word of it—so I couldn't have some kid banging
away at the wall while I moaned and slugged brandy under the
covers.

I'm wearing my flannel lounge pants and a gray T-shirt,
good enough for a brief trip to the untended Dumpster parked
down the street. The boxes weigh as much as stones. I prop
open the door to my studio before I pick one up, and when I've
lurched my way down the five narrow flights to the front door
I try to balance the thing on my hip while I yank the knob.
This doesn't work. I set the box on the third step, open the
heavy metal door, hold it with my right foot, lunge toward the
staircase with my left, reach for the box, pull it to my chest. By
the third box I'm a plaster ghost. I've changed the sanitary pad.
The brandy has worked its magic. My pelvis feels like a sunken
ship; there's pain there, but it speaks of distant battles, unrecov-
erable treasure; there's no point dwelling on it.

Trudging back upstairs, I run into Wally, the super. Wally's gangly, almost good-looking. Two teeth are rimmed in gold, and one of his eyes wanders. "This is the stupidest thing," I tell him, "I have ever done." I am referring to the demolished wall, of course. Wally doesn't know about the abortion.

"Have you knocked down the studs yet?"

I shake my head. "I look through them and think I'm in a jail cell. Why the hell was there ever a wall there in the first place?"

Wally nicks his head to the right, up the staircase. "I'll show you."

It was Wally and the guy downstairs, Neal, who helped get my mattress and box spring up the five flights. They were too wide to make the turns, so we pushed each of them straight up between the banisters. I broke three fingernails. The box spring's seen better days. It flew off the top of my car in a January blizzard as I was moving to the city from New Hampshire. I pulled over to the shoulder, dashed across four lanes, dragged the thing back, tried to lift it myself, gave up, put my hands over my face and burst into tears. When I paused for breath I heard a calm baritone saying "Ma'am? Ma'am? Do you need help?" It was an off-duty copy with a couple of spare bungees in his trunk. He hoisted, strapped, and went on his way.

Me and Blanche, I think as I'm headed up the stairs with Wally, my pad chafing between my thighs. Depending on the kindness of strangers.

My studio smells of blood and brandy, but Wally doesn't seem to notice. He heads over to one of my two rattling, dirty windows, hoists up the sash, and leans out. "There," he says when he's pulled his long frame back inside. A cold wind rushes through. Up the hill, on Park Avenue, the forsythia are in bloom, but people hurry by them with their scarves still wound tight. I lean out where Wally's pointing, into the wintry air. "See those braces?" he says behind me. Below, bolted into the brick, a series of L-shaped metal supports jigsaws up the side of the building.

"Yeah," I say as I pull my head back in.

"Those were for the ramp," he says. I look at him stupidly. I can still taste fermented blackberries, deep in my throat. "For the horses," he says.

"I've been living," I manage to respond, "in two horse stalls?"

I look around the studio. The wall is almost down. Faint traces remain of the joists that originally held it in place; it would not have run all the way to the ceiling. Evan, my archae-ologist husband, would love this. Just enough room, he'd point out, for two small fillies to turn around. At the ends where I now have my closet-sized bathroom and closet-sized kitch-enette, troughs for eating and drinking, a pile of hay. Every evening, up the ramp you go, Sunshine, five stories.

"The worst comes," Wally is saying behind me, "in the summer." He's glancing up at the ceiling, which is low, maybe seven feet. "The roof's tin," he explains. "You're gonna roast in here."

•

BEFORE WORK THE NEXT DAY, my phone rings. Good thing, since the brandy and loss of blood have dragged me to the bottom of a blackberry ocean of dreamless sleep. It's Betty Lou, our realtor in New Jersey. "The tenants are out," she reports, "and I've got exterminators lined up. They want someone at the house to sign off. I'm not going there."

"I know you're not, Betty Lou," I say. I'm up, moving, pulling work clothes off the portable rack that serves as my closet. "I've got some stuff to put in the attic. I'm driving out on Saturday."

"Okay, then. Just checking. I'll tell them noon."

"Noon's fine."

"I just don't know, with you people."

"It's fine, Betty," I say. With my free hand I'm pulling off the latest pad; not much bleeding. A fresh one from the plastic bin. "You can count on me," I say. "Just list the place, okay?"

"After this weekend," she says.

I skip the shower, skip breakfast, finger-comb my hair, take the subway. Already I'm exhausted. I can't afford another day off, though. I just started this job. The obscure branch of the State Department where I work is strategically located in New York, where business executives work and where they think about retiring. Our bosses here recruit them, as they shuffle away from their high-rise offices, to volunteer in countries recently converted to capitalism. If an enterprising fellow in such a country wants to start, say, a plastic-hat factory to put all the straw-hat-making peasants along the roadside out of business, we are their man. The retired executives get a nice suite in a four-star hotel and a per diem for themselves and their wives.

My job is to write up the reports of the projects and print them in blue ink on a single sheet of crisp bond. Aileen files them. Aileen is my one friend at work. She keeps a bottle of cheap red wine in one of the filing cabinets, and sometimes we stay after work and drink it out of coffee mugs. Aileen's the only one who knows why I was out sick for four days. Today's her thirtieth birthday, and the office is taking her out to lunch. This is Mr. Little's idea. Mr. Little—who is, in fact, little, a dapper white-haired man with a pencil mustache—has a crush on Aileen, though Aileen thinks he has a crush on me. Mr. Little is about eighty years old. His secretary, Faye, fixes his coffee every morning and brings it in to him on a little tray with a mini-pastry she's picked up from the French place around the corner. When I first came here, in January, I told Aileen I'd never worked anywhere with only male bosses who were addressed as "Mr." and only female employees who were addressed by their first names. "Wait till you see the Christmas party," she said.

Today isn't the Christmas party, but Mr. Little is wearing a red bow tie and even Aileen has left off her customary jeans for a pair of wool slacks and a silk blouse. After I've survived the morning, we gather at the Lebanese restaurant around the corner. Everyone orders Lebanese beer. I've eaten almost nothing in the past few days; by the time the falafel arrives, I'm a little tipsy. I start laughing with Aileen—who's sitting across from me, next to Mr. Little, positioned for the toasts we'll start making when everyone's passed the plates of food—about Middle Eastern cuisine and how ignorant we all once were. "When my husband first got to Beirut," I say, "he stayed at this B&B. That morning, he sits down at the breakfast table, and there's a bowl of garlic soup and a side of chopped raw meat. He figures that's what you eat so he starts in. And the wife rushes out at him, yelling that he can't, it's not American food, that's for her husband!"

"What does he get to eat?" Aileen asks.

I shrug. "Frozen bagel, I think," I say.

But Mr. Little is leaning our way. "I didn't know you had a husband," he says—a little louder than the rest of us, so his voice carries over the table and everyone shushes.

I feel my cheeks go red. "I didn't know I had to tell you," I say. And then, because I don't want to be rude, I add, "He's not really my husband anymore anyhow."

"I just never imagined you," says Mr. Little, and now he turns to the rest of the table, prepared to make some sort of pleasantry out of it, "with a husband."

I never imagined you with a wife, I want to say, but a look from Aileen shuts me up.

Let's get the messy part out of the way. The baby—what would have been the baby—was Evan's. We met in New Hampshire, at the fancy prep school where we both worked. We were together three years. I was on the Pill up to the last minute, or the last two months anyhow. I think it's fair to say that Evan and I hated each other, the way people tossed together on a desert island come to hate each other. I took to him because he was not (like Nick, like Marcus, like David) married. He took to me to prove he was not (like Q, the name I assigned his lover before me) gay. Bad idea on both sides, but there you were. Evan was headed away from the prep school to Princeton, for a doctorate in archaeology. We both quit our teaching jobs, and in June we made an offer on a little farmhouse ten miles from the university. The money came from Q, who'd died and left it all to Evan. Messy, right? By August, when we closed on the house, Evan had decided to defer for a year and go on a dig in Lebanon. Years from now, I predict, Evan will realize that I planted this idea in his head. Years from now, I may admit that he asked me, more than once, to come with him. Anyway, we rented the house and I spent four more months at the prep school coaching field hockey. When Evan came back for the holidays, I told him I was leaving New Hampshire, moving to New York. I said I didn't want to live so far away from everything all by myself. By the time he comes back in the summer, we won't hate each other anymore. I can help him move into the place or sell the place. We'll get a divorce.

I also told Evan, at Christmas, that I had gone off the Pill. I said there wasn't any point while he was 10,000 miles away. Not that there had been much point before. Yet the day before he left, he insisted on making love. I construed it as a fit ending. We coupled not on the bed but on the couch he'd inherited from Q. The whole time, I kept counting days from my last period. Safe, I kept telling myself, safe. Now when he comes back in June, dusty and satisfied, he'll remember that we held each other, that we loved each other, that we didn't hate each other, and we'll go our separate ways in peace.

Stupid. I know. So is living in two horse stalls. So is sleeping with Neal, which I started doing three weeks ago. So is trying to take down a wall slapped up with plaster over an old horse-stall partition. All through the lunch, Mr. Little shoots glances my way, because I've suddenly turned from a fetching young thing into a married woman, and he can't wrap his pencil-mustached mind around it. I've got a lot of mistakes left to go before I do something right.

"So you want to come with me," I ask Aileen as we're strolling back to the office, everyone convivial, "to Princeton this weekend?"

"You really in shape for that?" she asks with a quick glance to my belly.

Aileen is jonesing for marriage. She won't sleep with any of the bosses because they're married—smart girl—but she would take a retired widower if one moved into the corner office. Most of the time in the file room she's on Match. To her I am a cautionary tale. "I don't know what shape I need to be in," I say. "We're meeting exterminators. Carrying a few boxes to the attic. Be good to get out of the city."

"I've never been to New Jersey," she says and giggles.

•

FRIDAY NIGHT, NEAL COMES UPSTAIRS. I show him the supports for the horse ramp and tell him about the fillies. The boxes of plaster are gone, but I haven't gotten to the wood yet. "I'm thinking I'll leave it up," I tell him. "I'll tell people I live in a barn."

He lies flat on my bruised bed while I rub prescription cream into his back. Neal's back is covered with bumps and fissures, like moguls on a ski slope. Before he moved downstairs, a week ahead of me, he had been in a three-month coma after surviving a fire in his Chelsea loft. He thinks the girl he was sleeping with set the fire—she was crazy, he claims, and I don't ask more—and then got out. They found him unconscious from smoke inhalation, collapsed in front of the swollen door. Most of the skin into which I rub the greasy cream is from grafts.

Neal has a bland WASPy face, uninjured from the fire, and a way of looking a couple of millimeters left or right of your eyes. I don't trust him. I think he has another girlfriend. I picture him with his decadent pals cooking meth in the Chelsea loft. But February was a pit of loneliness, especially after the heat in the building shut off and I knew I'd counted the days wrong, back at Christmas. So when he started asking me to rub cream into his back I was happy to take things wherever they wanted to go.

"What happened to Jorge?" he asks. His hand strays to my leg.

"I had some medical issues. I had to use the money I was going to pay him with."

"You okay now?" The hand strokes my calf muscle.

"Not yet." With an ungreased pinkie finger I pull his wheat-colored hair back from his ear and kiss the lobe lightly. "But you don't really want me," I whisper. "I'm just the girl upstairs."

"I might move out," he says.

This news hurts in a way I won't acknowledge. I thumb the cream into the valleys between moguls. Neal has never objected to anything I've said. I tell myself I will remember his help with the mattress and how we needed each other's body heat to fall asleep in February. The rest will fall away. "When?" I ask.

"Summer maybe. It's sort of a share situation. But I haven't decided."

This is how we talk—share situation, medical issues. "I'll probably leave too," I say bravely. "Wally tells me I'll roast under this roof."

"You could move downstairs to my place, when I'm out."

What a sensible suggestion! I could dig my nails into Neal's scarred back. Instead, I picture my rage like smoke from a fire, sneaking through the cracks in the windows and wafting over the cold city. There, it's gone.

By the time I've finished creaming him, Neal's fallen asleep. I lie, clothed, on my side facing him and the demolished wall, my hand on his broad shoulder blades. I picture Mr. Little, propped up in bed next to his wife, both of them reading novels for their book clubs. He folds his across his lap and tells her about the report writer at work, how she turns out to be married. His wife can't understand what's so surprising. Girls do that, she teases him. They can't all be faithful just to you.

•

EARLY SATURDAY, I PICK UP AILEEN. I've rented a van from a lot near the Jackson Heights stop, and together we stop by the storage facility. In it I've stuffed Evan's stationary bike,

79

the frame backpack he lived out of for six months, his collection of Buddhist texts, the iron bedstead that once held the now-battered mattress and box spring, our kitchen table, and the infamous couch. The couch may have sentimental value for Evan, I don't know, but it's going to New Jersey. I'm feeling good. The taste of blackberry brandy is a lingering memory; the cramps have vanished; my jeans hang loose on my hips. There's a whisper of warmth in the air, the sky hazy, the flowers in the miniature gardens of Queens the fuzzy yellow of baby chicks.

"So glad to be getting out," says Aileen as we blast over the Verrazano. "My roommate Sandy? She's got this new guy, right? So he's over last night telling us about the girlfriend he had in L.A. who was raped by some prick she used to date, only they lost in court and the guy walked. So you know what? He *shot* the guy."

"You mean he kneecapped him, or—"

"No, I mean he *killed* him. With a .22, he claims. He says he wanted it to hurt. He says he was ready to do time for it but he never got caught. I mean this guy was in my *house*, Shelley, all right? He looks like a regular Queens guy, you know, a little Italian, a little clueless." Aileen shudders. "I wouldn't get in bed with him," she says.

I laugh, but it's nervous. "Did he ask?"

"No one is asking, you banana. I am a reluctant celibate. Wasn't that a movie or something?"

"'Reluctant Debutante.'"

"I wouldn't be reluctant there. That's who the rich guys marry. Debutantes. Djou see how Little bugged out at you at lunch the other day?"

"I don't see what difference it makes. I never think of myself as married."

"You say 'my husband.' People who don't think of themselves as married don't do that."

I don't answer. I'm trying to follow GPS. I haven't been down here since we closed on the house. Betty Lou was shocked

80

that we weren't going to move in right away. Evan kept saying, "Shelley'll keep tabs. I've got business out of the country. It'll all work out." Even when we were house-hunting, I knew buying a place together was a desperation move, the extreme gesture you make when you're on the precipice. "Let's not get divorced! Let's buy a house instead! Let's have a kid instead! Let's sail around the world instead!" Way over there in the Lebanese mountains, Evan thinks that the interest on Q's money is enough to pay residual expenses on the house, but he's wrong about that. I get the statements. Evan's been spending. When he gets back, he will have to find some income or sell the place. Meantime, Betty Lou has been calling with tenant complaints. There were rats, the tenants claimed. Running over their kitchen counters. Threatening their baby.

Now they've moved out, taking their security deposit with them, and the exterminator's moving in. Bye-bye to more of Q's money. I haven't told Aileen about the rats. I was thinking she was a tough cookie, a city girl. In the car, she's going on about this fellow with the .22, and I wonder if I should have brought her along. "You know, if you want to just wander around the town or something, while I take care of stuff at this house," I say as we leave the highway and start across the low hills.

"No way! I want to see your place. If it's nice enough, I might ask you to introduce me to this husband of yours."

"I don't think he'd be your type."

"Having a type is a mistake."

I was the one who found the house. Now, descending the long slope into the hollow, I'm shocked at how small and ordinary it looks. In keeping with the desperate nature of our foolishness in buying it, I had driven all over the county looking for just the place Evan would love, and I remember thinking, when I stepped into this Federal colonial—with its fenced yard so Evan could get a dog, and the neighbor's corn field rising up behind—that I had the ticket. Twenty minutes from the university, with a bright high-ceilinged study where

Evan could be a scholar; twenty minutes to the train, which I could ride to some esoteric employment three days a week in the city. Now it looks, despite the blazing forsythia, a little shabby. Across the road, two pickups are planted permanently in the neighbor's yard. But Aileen cries out, when we pull into the driveway, "Shelley, this is a dream palace! You want me to move in here with you?"

"You're what friends are for," I say, and step out.

It's weirder than I anticipated, sliding the key that's been on my ring since August into the back door lock. I own this place, half of it anyway. Evan and I planned where the furniture would go. We got the engineer's report on the rotting soffits. We negotiated with the sellers—a family, I'm recalling as I step into the sunlit kitchen, with a baby in a playpen, the mom talking strategically about the great daycare down the road—for the kitchen appliances, the washer and dryer in the basement. This is not a stranger's home. This is my house. And it's full, I remind myself as I hear Aileen mount the steps behind me, of rats.

"Better be prepared," I tell her.

"For what? I'm from Queens," she says.

Inside, the air's as cold as outside. I wonder if the furnace is on. I know just enough to fear frozen pipes. The kitchen's old fashioned—Linoleum floor, wooden cupboards, a blue plasticky counter surface, an electric stove with an analog clock stuck at 3:45. Down a step, an added wing for an eat-in nook, with windows on three sides. The frightened, litigious tenants have left the place clean. Gingerly I step toward the sink. Betty Lou had her assistant stop by and set traps in the likely places. I should find them before Aileen does. Quickly, as if for surprise, I pull on the C-shaped handle of the lower cupboard.

Two traps, both occupied by mice. Their bodies have gone flat, like tiny mouse rugs, their heads jutting grotesquely from the bar that snapped their necks. No maggots yet. I exhale. "There's mice," I tell Aileen. "That's why the tenants left."

82

I open other cupboards. Some traps are sprung, others occupied. I count 6 dead mice in all. The traps are big enough for rats, but no rat bodies bulge from the wooden planks. These vermin are shameless, the tenants have told Betty Lou. As I turn from the kitchen to the sitting room, I see one out of the corner of my eye. It scuttles from the bottom of the fridge to the bottom of the stove. A mouse. A tiny, quick field mouse.

"They got a stack of paper bags here," Aileen says. "You want me to scoop these buggers up?"

"You can do that?" I say.

She grins. "We got cockroaches bigger than this."

She's a good friend. I check the fireplace and close the flue; no point adding swallows to the menagerie. A braided oval rug, blue with brown, graces the center of the room, covering a stain in the wide boards that I remember noticing when we first looked at the house. We were going to sand and polish the floors upstairs and down. In 1870, I think, the house was built, a handsome little farmhouse, just late enough for the high ceilings. I duck around the main staircase to check out the study that was going to be Evan's. It's smaller than I remember, but with its own little fireplace, blocked off. "I'm going upstairs!" I call down to Aileen.

"Take your time!"

The steps to the second floor are steep and narrow, the carpeting worn. Upstairs the ceilings are lower—Evan had to duck his head through the doorways—and the windows begin a foot from the floor and go up to my chin. Faded wallpaper peels from the walls. We were going to strip it and paint. I inspect the plain bathroom, the two bedrooms. A window's been left open a crack; a sheer white curtain lifts in the draft. The south bedroom for us, the north for my study and later for the baby. In the baby's room the tenants have left a wooden chair with a broken strut. Carefully I sit in it and gaze out the window. Across the road, the neighbor's shaking a rug out the back door. She stands in the sun for a moment, getting its warmth on her face. She's maybe in her 40s. I think how I'll never know her, and I feel an ache at the back of my mouth. Three bikes in varying sizes lean against the front porch. I follow the woman's gaze across her yard in time to spot a horse amble from the stubbled grass into a ramshackle barn where it has its stall. No ramp.

From downstairs, Aileen calls: "I'm gonna start emptying the van, okay!"

"Great!" I shout back. "Be down in a sec!"

As I look out the dusty window of my house, I can feel it all happening. We've had the baby. Evan's finished his degree, I've done one kind of work or another. We've quarreled a lot. We've opened up the second chimney downstairs, and then closed it up again because it sucks too much heat from the house. We've stripped the wallpaper and painted, then five years later we've painted again, this time the eat-in kitchen after the remodel. I hate having just one bathroom, but building another down-stairs would take too much space out of the new kitchen. We've replaced our mattress twice and box spring once, but we've kept the iron bedstead, the paint chipping from the corner posts. The stairs don't seem steep to us anymore; other people's stairs seem shallow. I've come to know this house so intimately, like a lover's body. Its cracks and corners, its smells in all seasons. Every first frost, we get an influx of mice, then another in the spring when they come out of hibernation. We trap a bunch and keep the food sealed up, and for a while we keep a cat. Now and then, especially after the second child, we're tempted to move to a larger place, a newer place. But neither of us makes that much, and our friends come to love visiting us in this house, where we've built a wraparound deck looking over the side yard. Summer parties spill on to the grass. The children take carrots across the road to the filly, and later, when she's an old mare, they're allowed to ride her. Finally the girl and then the boy grow up and leave. Evan reclaims his study, or maybe I claim it this time. We don't think anymore about why we

84

married in the first place or why we quarreled so much. Vaguely I remember a moment in my life when I guzzled blackberry brandy in a plaster-strewn horse stall amid a damp and frantic Manhattan winter. I don't remember Neal at all, and I've lost touch with Aileen. When the kids are grown and the money worries ease up, we take a trip or two to those far-flung countries where the State Department sends retired executives, and we buy straw hats from the peasants by the roadside and wear them home. Sometimes, on weekends, we take the train into the city, and when we come back late at night the house is here waiting, smoky blue against the stars in a moonless sky.

Sitting on the broken chair, I feel this whole life I will never live pass through me and into the air of the house. I feel pretty happy with it all, even the difficult parts. For a moment that life is mine, mine and the house's. "All right," I say out loud.

Through the window I see a white truck pull into the driveway. Mice and cockroaches stare from its side walls through their cages, red circles with red slashes across the diameter. The exterminators are here to do their dirty, necessary work. I stand and descend the steep staircase, to help Aileen unload the van.

Concorde

JACKSON WAS ALREADY IN A BAD MOOD as he made his way through Concorde station. The klezmer band, which usually cheered him up, echoed through the corridors. Will trundled behind him with the grocery trolley. They'd been to the Marché Aligre, but Will hadn't liked it. Will preferred supermarkets, where he could pick things out for himself and didn't have to trot out his rudimentary French. As a result, since Will did the cooking, Jackson ate greasy chicken, rubbery steak, and vegetables picked weeks before they ripened. In France!

Jackson heard English spoken before he saw them: the blind guy and the two Brits at the bottom of the next stairway, shaking hands before parting ways. From the top of the steps he heard the blind guy say loudly, "Who speaks English and can help me?"

He didn't glance back to see how far Will was. He clattered down the steps. "I speak English," he said. "I can help you." He took the blind guy's elbow just like that, as if they were a couple about to head off to church. Behind them, the klezmer music faded.

"Thank you," said the blind guy. He had one of those white sticks, which he held like a leash, as if he were walking a dog. "I need to find the place where the door opens on the metro," he said. "On some cars, they open by themselves, and I can follow the sound. But if I find myself before a latched door, I don't manage to open it before the bell rings."

The blind guy spoke with a Middle Eastern accent. He had a soft, oval face, with a short brush of facial hair; back from his forehead, it was thinning. His eyes had the creepy unfocused look of all blind people.

"Here we are," Jackson said as the 12 train pulled alongside the platform. As he helped the blind guy cross the gap between platform and train, he glanced back. There came Will, through the next set of doors. Jackson tried to catch his eye, but Will gave him only a quick head nod before finding a seat and propping the market trolley between his legs. The car was packed. Along with the blind guy, Jackson stayed on his feet, gripping a pole.

Free to stare at a guy who couldn't see him, he put him at thirty years old, more or less; a few gray hairs were starting up among the dark brown. His eyes remained half-open, the pupils unfocused. He wasn't handsome. His lips seemed a little wet, full as a child's, halted in the midst of a smile. In the end, Jackson thought, you have to say something. "Where are you from?" he asked.

"I am from Iran."

"And what are you doing in Paris?"

"I am studying. My name," said the blind guy, "is Faisal." He shifted his white stick to the hand gripping the pole and held out his other hand, which Jackson shook briefly.

"Jackson," he said. He wished that Will were closer by. Will was a real teacher, the genuine article; every discovery of a student was like a gift for him. "What are you studying?"

"Actually, I am not studying yet. I need papers."

Ah. A refugee. A blind, undocumented Iranian in Paris. "But if you could study—"

"It would be massage," Faisal said—and as if he could see Jackson's surprise, "It is a good career, for a blind person. We are very good with our hands, and we do not embarrass the customers."

Jackson stole a look at Faisal's hands. Funny, how he tried to disguise his staring. The hands were fleshy and not strong-looking. But some people like a gentle massage. "And you're learning French?"

Faisal giggled, a girlish sound. They had stopped at

Madeleine to take on more passengers; the car had grown hot. Aboveground, the raw chill of early April. Jackson had two more months instructing American students in the niceties of Parisian architecture, then it was back to Buffalo and the dissertation that wouldn't quit. He'd grown up in Paris; that was why they'd come here on Will's sabbatical. Will, after all, was thoughtful; Will sensed how discomfited Jackson was on the wide, snowy streets of upstate New York; Will wanted him to feel at home for once. But the spoiled American students, the plastic-wrapped groceries fetched at Carrefour—that wasn't home. Lately, Jackson's life seemed like a play, with the charming Montmartre flat they'd rented as the stage set, and Will always on stage, reading philosophy and working on his book and cooking supper, while Jackson executed the exits and entrances. What Jackson really wanted was to send Will home, at the end of the semester, and relocate from their flat to a faceless *grenier* in the 11th arrondissement. He wanted to stay out until the wee hours at the bars by the Canal St.-Martin, smoking under the gas lamps while the football game played at the bar and the pretty boys came and went.

"I am trying," Faisal said. "But French is not an easy language, and I have no one to practice with. I find the Americans much friendlier than the French."

This recognition of being American, especially American in the age of Trump, this moment when his country was spreading shit around the world, always pained Jackson. When he wasn't with Will, he tried to pass for Parisian, but his language had slipped, and he suspected even his way of walking from the hip gave him away. "If you were to come to the States," he said, "you wouldn't find us so nice, I'm afraid. Our government isn't very welcoming, especially toward Iranians."

"And my government is even worse!" said Faisal, with the same high giggle.

At Gare St.-Lazare, the car shed half its passengers. There was room on the benches now, but Jackson and Faisal remained standing. Now and then, Jackson glanced back at Will. Will had pulled a journal out of the grocery cart—he always brought something to read—and was marking it with his pocket pen. His head tipped sideways, he wore his reading glasses. Will's whole demeanor, the social flesh that encased him as his pale skin encased his long muscles, was enviably smooth. Not impenetrable exactly; Jackson wasn't into men of mystery. Rather, like that Tempur-pedic material they used now for mattresses, a dense absorption of the other person that slowly vanished until nothing seemed to have pressed upon him. For five years now, Jackson had availed himself of Will's smoothness, had hurled at him every sharp spear of disappointment and seen it sink in, become absorbed and made invisible. He imagined sometimes that if he shook Will hard enough, all the slights, the barbs, the demands and disappointments would burst from his body.

"When we get rid of our government," Faisal said, "and you get rid of your government, we will get together. We will have a big party."

"That could take a while."

"It doesn't matter. We will find each other."

"Here in Paris."

"Oh yes! I will live here. Nothing will stop me."

"Can we bring friends?"

"All our friends. I will cook chelow kebab, the best you ever have had."

"And you'll be a massage therapist."

"I will give a massage to everyone at the party. Would you like a massage?"

"I would, actually. My lower back."

Faisal nodded as though he understood. They weren't flirting. Still, Jackson couldn't avoid the picture of himself, his white naked ass on the table and a blind men's soft fingers kneading. It lay just on the disgusting side of erotic, or maybe the erotic side of disgusting.

They pulled into Notre Dame de Lorette. "Do you know what stop you get off at?" Jackson asked. "Do you need help?"

"I get off at Pigalle. Two more stops. I count the stops, so I know."

"Well done." Pigalle, Jackson thought. He pictured a small, colorless room on the fifth floor. A bed, an overhead bulb, a microwave. Downstairs, the north Africans selling mobile phones and cocaine. Stench of fetid chicken and urine.

"I have the whole metro in my head," Faisal was saying. "I have the whole map of Paris in my head. I have so many things there. You cannot imagine," Faisal said, "how big my head is."

The car was close to empty now. At the other end, if he chose to, Will could hear everything they were saying. Faisal's smile had grown brighter, as if his eyes were turned inward and seeing the great expanse inside. At that moment Jackson knew this wasn't simply an undocumented refugee without resources, without hope. All the space that was filled, for Jackson, with images, friends, words on his computer screen—all of it could be cleared away to make room for a kind of knowledge that he had never touched before. "Clearly," he managed to say, "you'll get along well, here."

"Thanks to generous strangers, like you. You are so nice, Jackson. Your wife is very lucky."

Jackson hesitated. What the hell. One more stop. "I haven't got a wife. I've got a boyfriend. He's here, in the car with us." He glanced back at Will. Sure enough, he was looking now. Jackson's hands began to sweat. "He's got our grocery cart," he said.

"He is a lucky person," Faisal said. "You are a kind and handsome man."

"You can't see me."

"Your voice is handsome. Your children will have a great father."

Jackson's mind rang with confusion. "If I ever have them," he managed to say, "I'll call you to come tell them so."

"And I will do it, because it will be true."

All through this exchange, Faisal smiled gently with his wet lips. He was saying the things that a person in his home country always said to a woman. Six years ago, Jackson had gone on a month-long dig in Egypt. He recognized the tropes—you asked a woman about her children, you assumed she was married, that she did whatever she did with the consent of her husband. Faisal had begun with the assumption that Jackson was a husband; then he had made him a wife. Jackson ought to resent it.

The P.A. system began the announcement. *Pigalle?* It was always framed as a question, the initial mention of the next stop. When you broke into the station, the question became a statement—as if, Jackson always thought, the métro was unsure where it would arrive until it got there. *Concorde? Concorde. St. Paul? St. Paul.*

"This is my stop," said Faisal. "I feel we have become great friends."

He lifted his blind face, and Jackson kissed him, first one bearded cheek, then the other. He felt the brush of Faisal's full lips on his jaw.

Pigalle.

"We will have this party, Jackson," Faisal said as he turned to lift the handle on the door.

"How will you find me?" Jackson said.

"I will find you."

"Wait. Here," Jackson said, and he reached for his wallet and pulled out one of the cards he'd had foolishly printed, when he began the stint at the study-abroad program. He tucked the card into the pocket of Faisal's loose raincoat. "So you'll remember me," he said. But the door had closed by then. In any case, he realized as the métro pulled away and he watched the blind man tap his way down the platform with his white cane, Faisal couldn't read any text other than Braille.

Three more stops. He took a seat next to Will. Without lifting his eyes from his journal, Will reached up and scratched the back of Jackson's head. "You okay?" he asked.

91

"Sure," Jackson said. He loosened the cord on the market trolley and peeked inside. "I'm sorry I made you buy all this," he said. "You don't have to cook it."

"You can show me how. When in Paris and all that."

Jackson looked out at the blinking lights. Then he shut his eyes. He pictured the tunnel boring deep below Sacré-Coeur, twisting sharply to the right at Lamarck. Below Paris, he had learned in his childhood, lay a catacomb almost as big as the city itself, hollowed by the limestone excavated to erect the great buildings of the city. An entire society thrived down there. They slept in crawl spaces. They staged nightclubs, complete with jazz bands and sultry altos, in vaulted caves. Maybe that was what Faisal saw, inside the huge gallery of his head. "We should have him over," he said.

"Who? That blind guy?" Will chuckled. "You'll never see him again."

"He'll find me. We have a date. For a party." He opened his eyes. He turned toward Will, who practically glowed with loneliness. He laced their fingers. "You're invited," he said.

Foreign Climes

KATE WORKED IN ONE OF THOSE GRAY EUROPEAN CITIES whose monstrous eighteenth-century buildings abide within cages of scaffolding. Over its cupolas and steeples hovered the maws of bright yellow cranes. Everything was being restored: halls of justice, fountains, Doric columns, statues of long-forgotten soldiers and poets. In the few vacant lots where history had gnawed out the root of the old civilization, towers of glass and onyx loomed like spears hurled down from another planet, warning the natives.

Winter was passing for her, had passed almost, in a damp miasma of dog droppings and soiled newspapers backed against the deserted circular fountains. All the unrestored cast-metal statues sported a chartreuse green. Kate wondered frequently, repetitiously, whether their casters had been aware of the properties of copper carbonate, whether they had planned for centuries of empire-supported polishers to keep the copper shiny. Perhaps they hadn't minded the onset of this druggy green, sign of seniority.

Seagulls circled above the leathery surface of the pond she passed daily. Truck vendors sold sausage sandwiches and fried potatoes with spicy mayonnaise dressings, which Kate bought for a shiny coin and ate with a thin red plastic fork. The first bite burned the roof of her mouth, and the last tasted of the animal grease in which everything was cooked. She noticed these things. She was falling in love, and it scared her.

•

THE SMALL, PLEASANT OFFICE where Kate worked sat at the bottom of steep granite steps that led from the massive city hall to the theatre district. Kate's job was to appraise antiques for

93

export to the United States. She had arrived here, three years ago, because she was having an affair with the export manager. When he died in a car accident shortly after her arrival, she had stayed on. The firm liked her work—she had a careful eye, and a kind manner with the old ladies whose crystal she rejected—and Personnel managed somehow (she didn't ask) to renew her papers each year. And each year she stayed, though summer passed hesitantly and winter made her think always of the wars this city and others like it had barely survived. Lines for bread, she thought; dung burned for fuel.

She spoke the language passably. Once a week or more she was invited to a dinner party at which others her age—bureaucrats, young lawyers, antique dealers—chatted excitedly around her and she soaked up their energy like a sponge going red with the excellent wine. Her thoughts felt simple to her on these occasions. The vocabulary at hand contained none of the shadings she was used to. In the empty, half-sober moments after she'd returned to her flat, she wondered sometimes if her party companions thought simple thoughts—but that was her American prejudice at work, filtering out whatever subtleties it couldn't immediately process. She went to bed with the vapor of mystery. What did anyone think, really, and was language just a bowl to contain it? On rare occasions she missed the manager who had brought her here, the one who had died on a hairpin turn in the neighboring mountains. But she had scarcely known him, when you got down to it, and the years had smudged him into the gray of the city, until when she dreamed of him he was speaking in this other language, the one that made thoughts simple.

She fell in love not at a party but at a sidewalk stand, the one nearest her office, where she waited in spring mist for a grated lamb sandwich and a can of beer to make her lunch. The man in front of her spent his waiting time fooling with a fancy pocket calculator. He seemed nervous, and she thought maybe she would help him, when his turn came, with the strange names of the sandwiches. The day was windy, she would remember later; it had been windy for more than a week, and her hair was going tangled and coarse at the ends. She had learned to tie a scarf around her neck like the local people, but she would not wear their loose-knitted hats.

He ordered a large sausage sandwich with Andalousian sauce, a beer, and a package of pork rinds. He placed the order fluently, in the slack dialect of men who depend on such food, and he adjusted what she noticed were large hands to carry it all to one of two splintery green benches in the small park by the food stand. By the time she made her way to the other bench, he had spread his lunch on either side and was eating calmly in the wind with a thick text spread over his knees. He wouldn't spill a drop of grease on his neat pants and sweater, she thought, and she practiced the phrase in the local language a few times before she realized, suddenly, that she had said it, aloud and in English: "I bet you won't spill a drop of grease on those pants."

"I've spilled plenty in the past," he said. He didn't look up. He spoke like someone from the Midwest. "One learns."

"Your book won't flop closed, either. Mine always flops closed, if I don't have a hand free."

"You have to choose heavy pages." With a long pinky, he turned the page, then looked over. His lips were full and almost feminine, shining a bit with the oil from the sandwich. "There are restaurants," he said.

"I'm inside all morning."

"You work here, then?"

She nodded in the vague direction of her office. He didn't even glance, but smiled cunningly, as if he'd already mapped the route. "This isn't a city, you know," he said, crunching a pork rind. "It's a work zone."

"Will they ever finish, do you think?"

He shrugged. "They restored the Coliseum. And those were Italians."

"They have better weather."

He said something she didn't understand.

"What?"

"Polish saying. 'Plant in the rain and the roots grab hold.'" He pushed the last of the sandwich into his mouth and washed it down. Closing the book, he stood and wiped his hands on his paper napkin. (Where had he gotten that napkin? They never gave her one, at the stand.) Then he reached into his inside jacket pocket and pulled out a card. *J. Roscher*, it read. *Simultaneous translation & interpretation. French, German, Dutch, Italian, Polish, English.*

•

HE TOOK HER FIRST TO AN INDIAN PLACE several blocks into a questionable district of the city, where they ate papadums and a lightly saffroned, greaseless lamb. (She initiated the phone call, though not the rendezvous. She invented the pretext of needing to translate a Dutch inscription on a silver bowl.) Next they tried a very expensive, tiny Japanese pocket where he selected varieties of raw fish that she never knew swam in the sea. At the third restaurant, his neighborhood favorite, a round fussy woman prepared them both chicken waterzoi and plied them with a bright green aperitif while they waited. Kate got up her courage to ask about his scar, a neat slice in the shape of an acute accent running from his left earlobe toward his prominent Adam's apple. She had not noticed it the first day, at the lunch stand, but as he swallowed and spoke, she found her eyes straying there.

"A memory," he said, tasting the excellent though slightly sweet wine he'd ordered, "of my roustabout days."

She loved the way he used slang, not inappropriately, but with the imagination of someone who has discovered rather than inherited. The picture of Joaquim—that was his given name, not quite compatible with the "J." of the card—with his pursed lips and fair forehead, as a roustabout, made her laugh.

"I almost died," he said.

"I'm sorry."

"That's quite all right," he said. "Anyhow, I lived."

Smiling at him over the narrow rim of the aperitif glass, Kate realized she had begun dreaming about Joaquim's face and body, the slouch in his posture, the sleepy weight of his eyelids, the hair he combed straight back from his high forehead, like a symphony conductor. That night he came back with her to the ground-floor apartment she had been renting since the export manager's death, and they made love with a competence that, at least on Kate's part, just managed to hint at her wild rush of feeling. While they were at it, Joaquim murmured to her in German, French, Italian, Polish, and one other language that could have been Danish or Norwegian. Later he lay with a hand cupping her breast and told her a funny story in English about the first American girl he had known, who had exclaimed over the shape and behavior of his uncircumcised penis.

"How," Kate asked sleepily, suffused with love, "do you hold all those languages in your head?"

"How does a mother hold all her babies in her arms?" he asked her back. "How does a criminal hold all his crimes in his conscious? How does a composer hear all the instruments of the symphony?"

Kate did not answer; she was not supposed to answer. She was supposed to lie with her head on Joaquim's bony chest and smell the wine-sweetened exhalations of his pores. Only as she drifted off to sleep did she catch his error. *Conscience*, he had meant, not *conscious*. The kind of mistake that even a native might make.

•

WHAT SCARED HER WERE THE SILENCES. What she knew about Joaquim might have explained them. He had been born, he told her, in Holland, but had moved to Paris with his mother, who took up with a Polish diplomat. They lived five years in Chicago. "And the rest, as they say, is history," he said, twirling a lock of Kate's trimmed hair.

Silence was the space between one language and another, the place of memory. But that explanation, for Kate, didn't suffice. She wanted to know what he was really. She watched him sleep and wondered what language he dreamed in. When he spent the evening at her flat, he brought classical CDs and sat listening to Palestrina or Messiaen. She could cook or watch the news or sit with him, holding his hand, but he would not hold up his end of a conversation. He wasn't angry, he told her, or bored. He was just emptying his reservoir of words, drifting back to the original *da*.

Out in the world, he was full of words. The international courts kept him on retainer; he also translated sometimes for visiting theatre troupes and TV crews. In his spare time, he was translating World War I accounts from Italian into German. Thus the heavy tome, which he had been reading in the wind, and the calculator, which was a translation device.

As the days warmed they went biking together, through the beech forest just outside the city that had once been the king's domain. The paths criss-crossed, dead-ended, climbed around hills and dove into gullies. The sun, out at last, glinted through the tall beeches, their leaves lime green. Once they took lunch at a former cloister in the midst of the woods, where people much taller and more beautiful than Kate's co-workers sat with their large sleek dogs at outdoor wooden tables drinking Abbey beer and rosé wine and eating open-faced peasant sandwiches of white cheese sprinkled with radishes and onions. Ten feet from them, new families of ducks and coots, hoping for tosses of bread, cruised the edge of the pond once used by the monks as a fishery. The baby coots had bright red beaks and pushed their heads along, pigeon-like, imitating their stern bourgeois parents.

"*Comme tu es belle dans cette lumière,*" said Joaquim. "*Wie schön du bist in dieser licht. Sei bella alla luce—*"

"I get it," Kate interrupted. He looked hurt. "I'm sorry," she said.

98

"No problem. It is hard to switch gears. You look lovely, in this light."

"Thank you, darling," she said.

He turned his attention to the pond and took a long draught of his beer. "Watch the egret," he said. He gestured with his beer glass toward a thin gray bird stepping daintily around the brick wall edging the pond. Leaning his long neck over the side, the bird came up with a small fish, which he wriggled down. Suddenly there was a movement high in a willow tree. "Ah," said Joaquim.

"What? What's in the tree?"

"The fellow who got here first," said Joaquim.

A larger egret swooped out of the thick branches. He made a pass at the fishing bird, then landed on the far side of the pond.

"Maybe they're male and female," Kate said, watching the near egret jump away to take refuge in the overhang of another willow. "This could be a mating ritual."

"Dream on, Polyanna," said Joaquim, and she tucked that one, *Polyanna*, away to ask him about later. The larger egret stalked the pond. The other patrons were watching now. One woman had pulled a video recorder out of her large bag. Soon, as the newcomer wandered out of his haven, the big egret launched a stealth attack, flying low and straight over the surface of the pond. At the last moment, while Kate held her breath, the newcomer took to the air. The birds climbed, glided, flapped, turned. Faster on account of his wider wing span, the pond's defender kept coming up on the intruder from below, his beak out, ready to peck belly or wing. They flew through the fountain in the middle of the pond, over the willows; they pivoted as sharply as they could. The woman with the video camera kept squeaking, but Kate could not make a sound.

Finally, the bigger egret chased away the newcomer—first to a willow tree that shook with its weight, and finally away from the pond, out over the vast beech woods. Then the winner sloped down to a rock, gave a little shiver, and posed, immobile, on one leg.

"Now," said Kate, "he'll be all alone."

"That's how he likes it," said Joaquim.

"I was rooting for the littler guy," she said. She took a bite of her white-cheese sandwich. She could taste the rye field in the bread, the milked cow in the cheese.

"It is all about territory," he said. And then in an undertone, not meant for her to hear, *Es gibt immer am heimat. Tu chodzi o ziemiz.*

That night they ate oysters at his apartment, a tidy, elegant top story of a family house. His Italian war volumes lay scattered about the sitting room. CDs of chamber and orchestral music—no voices—lined the shelves. From the open window to the balcony came the throaty lyric of the local nightingale. Down below lay the tiny, carefully partitioned gardens that ran behind the tall houses, the length of the block. Kate pictured lifting the brick walls that separated them, the way one might lift the cardboard honeycomb of a wine case, and letting the gardens run together in a lush city forest.

Later she lay awake, watching his face move through sleep. She herself had dreams in which she spoke her second language perfectly, without accent, and her thoughts in these dreams were as thick and beveled as crystal, though they vanished when she woke.

•

SHE WENT TO WATCH HIM WORK. He had promised her it would be dull. He sat in a glassed booth at one of the courts, where one fishing industry took another's dumping practices before the bar, or one country's pharmaceuticals objected to another's patenting practices. This litigation had to do with exporting antiques from the European Union, an issue in which she might take a passing interest. "Passing!" exclaimed Kate.

On the first truly hot day of summer, she took an afternoon off work. Dressed in an uncharacteristic sleeveless dress of bleeding blue madras, she rode the subway to the end of the line and then stood by the city's outer wasteland of industry to catch a rumbling bus to the glassed-in complex that held the courts. On the bus, which was crowded, several men glanced approvingly at her. Kate had grown prettier since falling in love. Her export manager had liked her for her youth and competence and possibly for her hair, which in good weather hung in thick chestnut curls just over her shoulders. But she had been shy back then, and since his death she had taken to hunching her shoulders in what seemed the constant chill of the city. She no longer looked American—she never walked from the hip as the American tourists did, nor did she raise her voice above the other commuters on the subway. But on this ride out to the halls of European justice, she stood tall in her foreignness. She was like the new buildings, designed by architects from the Orient or California, and not like the crabbed and crutched representatives of a vanished empire.

Joaquim had left her name at the desk. The stern woman who sat there took her passport and gave her a nametag. Huge modern paintings hung on the high blond walls of the corridors; it felt more like an auction house than a courthouse. She made her way up to the fourth floor and down a long gallery to a set of heavy wooden doors, where a coterie of dark-suited men stood conferring. A pair of them glanced at her. She smiled apologetically and slipped inside the chamber.

There was a fair crowd of spectators. A few sat straight and listened to the proceedings—three judges at the front and lawyers with documents and arguments in what Joaquim had told Kate would be Polish. The others sat hunched on the long benches with headphones plastered to their ears. The nationality bringing the case, Joaquim had explained, was allowed to argue in its own language—and sure enough, two of the three judges had their own earphones, like odd wigs. The respondents could argue in that same language or in either French or English. All arguments and opinions would be translated into nine languages, fourteen if the matter involved the constitution of the European Union.

All these things Kate understood. But as she slipped into one of the pews toward the back of the room, the silence and strangeness felt more alien to her than anything she had encountered in her three years of living abroad. The lawyer arguing gestured mightily with his hands but spoke in a hurried, muted Polish directed at the one judge without earphones. That judge would nod, or lift an eyebrow, and perhaps five seconds later, as the translation came through the other judges' earphones, they would mimic her gesture.

Before she reached for the black headpiece dangling from a hook at her knees, Kate scanned the elevated glass booths at the front of the courtroom. There, in the third one, sat Joaquim. He, too, was gesturing, with even more alacrity and purpose than the lawyer. He kept putting the tips of his fingers to his forehead and then letting them spring away, as if he had yanked a difficult thought from his brain. *Deutsch*, a white label on his booth read. Kate clapped the earphones on her head and turned the dial to German. There was Joaquim's voice, no mistaking it: the rising vowels, the almost undetectable lisp, the emphatic schwas. But the intensity of his voice was something altogether different. She was used to light irony, to coy allusions and elliptical phrasing. Even without understanding the German, she knew from the voice coming through the headpiece and the body movements of the man in the glass booth that he meant every word he said.

Kate turned the dial to the next language, Italian, and scanned the booths. She matched a woman to the voice, a plump olive-skinned matron with her hair in a bun. Like Joaquim, she gestured, but her words were less fluid, more full of stops and rushed starts. Kate turned again, to English. *Following Section Three of the 1973 accords*, the male voice said, *these transactions are in keeping with the—with the fundamental principle of estate sales and free distribution. Museum purchasing is entailed by Section Five Part Three. There we have granted the plaintiff his remedy. Here in specific we are talking about Louis Quinze jaundiced intaglio.*

Not *jaundiced*, Kate thought. He must have meant *varnished*. The translator—a balding fellow in the booth nearest her, who kept adjusting his round glasses—sounded British, but then Joaquim could sound American. Perhaps the two words, *jaundiced* and *varnished*, sounded the same in the original; or perhaps the lawyer had used another word that meant yellowing, and the translator had come up with *jaundiced* before he understood the meaning of the whole sentence, and now it was too late. The words tumbled on. "The worst," Joaquim had told her, "is German into French or English. You have to hold the entire sentence in your head until the speaker finally lands on that darn verb at the end, and then you recite it all in order while the speaker goes right on to the next subject."

"That darn verb," Kate had repeated, and looped her arms around him.

The arguments dragged on. Spectators came and went. It seemed the Poles bringing the case believed that lost Jewish treasures, just now uncovered, were being plundered without regard for the butchered culture they represented. But the arguments waxed more technical. In the glass booths, after a half-hour, new translators entered from the back, clapped headphones over their ears, adjusted their microphones, and between one breath and the next, relieved the one who had been at the task. When Joaquim left his post, Kate rose and exited to the wide, hushed corridor.

Joining her, Joaquim pressed a hand into the small of Kate's back and steered her to the elevator and down into a small courtyard ringed by the building. He looked ravaged; as soon as they were outside he pulled out his pack and lit a cigarette. They sat at a small iron table. The sun had gone behind a scrim of clouds, and Kate shivered in her blue dress. Joaquim leaned over, smoke in his breath, and kissed her.

"So what do you think?" she said.

"About what?"

"This case. It seems to me they've got a point. No one's brought found estates to us yet, but I'd think we'd pause before shipping anything abroad. There ought to be laws."

Joaquim looked at her intently. "Katerina," he said, "I don't know anything about the case."

"Well, neither do I, really, but just from what you were saying—"

"I don't even know what I was saying." He drew on the cigarette and stared at a corner of the courtyard. "It's just words," he said. "As soon as I hear them I must remold them. I get them to make sense in German—"

"Or French. Or English."

"Yes, or Italian, and then they leave me while the other words are pouring in. My dear, I know less about 'the case' than the mouse who nibbles in the corner."

"Oh," said Kate. Then there seemed nothing more to say. Joaquim smoked. Just when she thought he was annoyed with her, he took her hand. His warm fingers stroked her palm. Tentatively, she reached out and touched his scar, which was no more than a rough indentation on his neck.

After ten minutes, he glanced at his watch. "Time for me to go back in," he said.

"And make with the words again," said Kate.

"Yah. And make the words."

•

SHE BEGAN BRINGING JOAQUIM WITH HER to the little soirées her friends had. He conversed readily, if not at length. Her friends, for their part, accepted Joaquim as one of their own. It was only as they were walking home through the long, late twilight, that Kate felt her lover shedding the conviviality of the evening like a coat that had grown too heavy for the warm air.

"If you don't like them," she said at last, "we don't have to go, next time."

But they did go. And Kate would introduce herself to a new arrival: "Yes, I'm American. And Joaquim is—well, I guess Joaquim is everything. Or nothing." The new person would laugh indulgently, and Joaquim would smile patiently, and Kate would glow.

"You should see where he works," she found herself explaining one night. "It's this complete Tower of Babel, only disassembled. I mean, there they are discussing stolen Jewish property from the Holocaust, for God's sake, and Joaquim here is politely translating from Polish into German."

"What would you rather?" asked the person she was speaking to. "That he go to war over the past?"

"No! Only there should be substance, don't you think? Not just strings of legal terms."

They turned to Joaquim, who smiled thinly. "Much," he said, "gets lost in translation."

To her own surprise, Kate was becoming at once comfortable and cruel. She pushed for a raise at work and began to dress like the people they had seen in the Abbey garden. She corrected Joaquim when he used *lay* for *lie* or claimed to be hungered. She walked taller and laughed louder.

In short—Kate told herself frequently—she had changed.

•

WHEN SHE BROKE OFF WITH HIM, she told her friends at one of the soirées that she could be with someone who thought in another language, but not with someone who thought in no language at all. She was speaking more fluently, by then. The words she had adopted had become plastic. She could say one thing and mean another, or mean two things at once. She cracked jokes, told stories about her childhood. For a short time she dated the retail manager at a rival export house, a square-jawed soccer player who had grown up in the city.

Through the cool, damp summer, she looked occasionally for Joaquim at the sidewalk lunch stand. He had not seemed hurt by the breakup. He had regarded her thoughtfully and kissed her tenderly and said almost nothing. She dreamed several times of his scar, of how he had gotten it—a bar fight in Chicago, a near escape as a spy in Poland. And then she thought of him little, until the scaffolding came down on the little theatre near her office.

All through one lunch she watched the workers bringing down the tiers of planks and ropes and metal tubing, their teamwork a delicate dance of climbings and lowerings. The day was windy, like the day she had met Joaquim, only it was autumn blowing in now. The workers had to step carefully, once the guard rails came down.

Underneath the scaffolding, the theatre had been scraped and whitewashed, its cornices replaced, its windows refitted. Over the door, a polished brass Cupid aimed its bow at pass-ersby, who turned to point. Kate wanted to tell someone in her office how the theatre looked like a newborn baby, fragile and robust at once. But she knew them, the locals and the Americans. Like most antique dealers, they preferred the new. The theatre with the scaffolding and the theatre restored looked more or less the same to them.

Next day, leaving work early, Kate took the bus back out to the industrial park and the international courts. The woman at the desk would not give her a pass—but yes, she said, Mr. Roscher still worked here. Kate left a message and then waited in the lobby, under a large abstract oil that made her think of Pick-up Sticks.

When she saw him, he was deep in conversation with the carefully coiffed translator she had seen in the Italian booth. They were speaking Italian, obviously—Joaquim used his hands in the Italian way, folding the air in front of him like pasta dough. When they reached Kate they kissed cheeks and called "Ciao," and Joaquim sat next to Kate on the cushioned bench.

"So," he said, his English still slightly inflected by Italian, "you have flown back to my territory."

"Have I?" Kate looked around. The courts were letting out. Soon all the languages of the Old World would pass by her bench. "Then you must chase me away," she said.

"But you are female."

"More important," she said, "I am not an egret."

"What are you, then?"

"I think," she said, shifting her hips to turn toward him on the bench, "I am a crane."

"Then I am a crane."

"Or perhaps I'm a heron."

"My legs are long and blue."

"I think, actually," said Kate, "my mother was a swallow."

"We are good luck for newlyweds, we *hirondelles.*"

"But I must know what sort of bird you are really, before I dare enter your territory."

Joaquim's face, this close up, was a landscape of pores and laugh lines, his beard a newly planted field. On his breath Kate smelled cheap mints, and under them beer and sausage.

"The funny thing about birds," Joaquim was saying, in Kate's adopted tongue, "is that the newest species are often confused with those that are almost extinct. They remain difficult to classify."

"What song do you sing?"

"Our species," he said, "utters a lyric so rare and strange that ordinary ears cannot hear it at all."

"So they mistake it for silence?"

Joaquim nodded, the scar on his neck contracting. Kate closed her eyes. Her ears opened. She strained at first, then simply waited, to hear.

From the Roof

THE NEXT DAY, AFTER WORK, Nadia drove to the stretch of highway where Kristof had done it. On one side rose the bleached white towers of the paper-bag factory; the other, as well as she could make out through the streaming cars, was fenced-off swamp. Wetlands, they would call it now. From the shoulder where she'd pulled off she smelled gasoline exhaust and the tangy chemicals of the factory. Up to now the place had meant nothing to her. She lived on the other side of town, in the foothills.

There would be jokes about it, of course. Watch for low-flying Airedales. If you can read this, do you know where your dachsund is? Seatbelts save bitches.

They had kept dogs, when Kristof was little. Three of them, ranging in size like the kids—a big golden lab for Hanna, a spaniel mix for Kristof, a fox terrier for little Lili. When Kristof was manic he'd come home from school and throw himself on the floor with the animals. "Oochy koochy parlee voo!" he'd cry out, a gangly kid of sixteen. "Bobbo, Anders, Peewee, my buddy wuddies!" They'd plant their paws on his chest and lick his face; he'd even open his mouth for them. Peter thought it was disgusting and said so, but you didn't cross Kristof, in those moments. You planted a sort of fence around him, and hoped it held.

Nadia had the latest news this morning from the radio, which she liked to keep on in the kitchen. "*Weird* accident out on 44," the announcer had said in his adenoidal voice. "Some local sociopath held a pure-bred Pomeranian responsible for his fender bender, and ordered the pooch's execution by tossing him into traffic. Animal rights activists are *incensed*. The Pom's owner, Melinda Mayhew of Baxterville, told police she had just rolled down her

108

window when a large white man reached in for the dog, who liked to ride on her lap. She reported the car as a red SUV. Says here she caught the first three characters of the license plate, which are EXT. That's as in 'extension,' folks, and if this guy is an extension of anything, it's his own Rottweiler personality."

Later there was a panel discussion, but Nadia wasn't listening. Already she'd gone out to inspect the Cherokee, though she knew it was red, and its plate read EYT478, which was close enough. The back fender was newly nicked, a giant thumbprint in the metal. Kristof was in the basement, watching *X Files*. She marched downstairs. "They're looking for you," she said in Polish.

"No shit," said Kristof, in English. John Lithgow was turning slowly around on the screen, a mocking puzzlement on his face.

"I think you should turn yourself in."

"Well, I don't."

"Kristof, look at me. Are you off your meds?"

"No," he said falsetto, "I am not off my effing meds."

Nadia's eyes had burned as she shut them. "We will talk about this later," she'd said. "I'm going to work."

When he was twelve, when they started with just Depakote, Kristof amazed her by swallowing the smooth pink pill each time she handed it to him. He hated it, but he swallowed it. If he didn't, she would take him back to the doctor. It broke her heart, the first few times, to see him so innocently pop the drug. It wasn't until they added the Lampresal that meds became a battle of wills. Kristof hated the weight gain, the nausea, the way he dropped asleep at his desk. He was off his meds the summer he came home from college and the spaniel died. He slammed doors so hard that the one to the bathroom cracked. Then—yes—that was one of the roof walks. Kristof at the gutter, two stories up, his arms splayed out like an angel. And you never knew, you just never knew when despair might lift its wings, and so she stood on the gravel drive and pleaded, she sent Lili to call 911, she endured the neighbors. The next day they had buried the pooch, and Kristof had been calm as a stone.

A breeze kicked up the stink of the swamp. Nadia turned her head. Shit for brains, *gówno*, Kristof would have called the woman who bumped him. Standing outside her driver's window, while she buzzed it down. Then the grab at what lay in her lap, its little pink mouth panting, and the fling across the single lane, to where the traffic whined. Well, he was mad. Anyone would be. He dealt with this patch of road every day, on his way from the bike shop where he'd found work. They needed a four-lane here, everyone said so. Forty miles an hour, and always some chuffing truck followed by a conga line. How many people, if they could grab something small and alive and hurl it, just to make something *happen*—how many wouldn't be tempted? Kristof was different only in this way: he acted.

The woman's mouth in a perfect O. The dog silent, its paws out, wondering if this is a new trick, ready to land on his white feet. And the traffic moving now, like a drain unclogged, drivers behind honking, get going, Kristof speeding away.

•

AT THE CRUNCH OF GRAVEL, Nadia lifted her head. A van drew up behind her Taurus. A middle-aged couple got out and opened the hatch. After they pulled out what seemed to be a roll of plastic, the man looked over at Nadia. A ponytail cinched his thinning gray hair; his Greenpeace T-shirt was unevenly bleached. "Awful, isn't it?" he said—loudly, over the noise of traffic.

Nadia nodded. "Hard to believe," she said.

The woman, also ponytailed, was tying one end of the banner to the fence bordering the factory grounds. "That murderer," she said conversationally, "ought to be strung up by his testicles."

She lisped a little, saying the word. Her partner tied the other end. The banner was black, with a picture of a white poodle's head. The tears that dropped from the poodle's eyes weren't very convincing, but the large blue type reading simply "Man's Best Friend..." did the trick.

"To be realistic," said Nadia, "if they do catch him, what can

110

they do to him? I mean, there must be laws," she added when the woman's eyes widened.

"He gets convicted of extraordinary cruelty to an animal," said the man, "he'll do time." He stepped back to admire his handiwork. The banner fought the fence in the breeze. From passing cars came a few windy shouts of encouragement. Then another car, rusted blue, pulled over.

"Amazing, isn't it?" said the driver who stepped out. He raised a camera to his face, squinted, and clicked. Both Nadia and the ponytailed couple stepped back, as if the lens were a weapon. "For the newspaper," the photographer explained, stepping around the car with his right hand outstretched. He was close to Nadia's age, lanky and badly dressed.

"We have a public relations office," said the woman.

"Don't wait for them." Her husband reached into his back pocket and handed the photographer a bent brochure. "Spread the word. Get the bastard," he said, and jerked his chin upward.

"Thanks, fella," said the photographer. He handed around his card. *Dean Dexter*, it read. *Press-Advocate*. "I mean, it is news," he said, mostly to the two women. "Man bites dog, practically."

"There's to be a burial tomorrow," said the woman. She had drawn closer to her husband. Cars whipped by; children pressed their noses to the window, hearing their parents tell the awful story as they passed.

"Burial?" Dean Dexter jotted a note.

"Beau Repos Pet Cemetery," said the man. "Behind the K-Mart, on Route Ten, at 5:30. They're donating the plot."

"That poor Miss Mayhew," said the woman.

"Mayhew?" echoed Nadia, momentarily perplexed.

"Yeah, we got her name," said the ponytailed man. "Now all we need's his."

•

NADIA DROVE BACK THROUGH TOWN, the highway widening as the buildings crowded closer together. Local economy had slipped since they'd moved here with Peter, the year Lili was born. In those days, the bag factory was hiring, and there was also a cutlery manufacturer, famous since the turn of the century. But the cutlery people had gone out of business, and the paper bag makers sent a third of their work overseas.

Every so often Nadia received a note from Peter, who now lived in Baltimore. He kept in touch with Lili; the other two, he had pointed out gently, weren't his. For Nadia he would enclose some newspaper clipping he'd found pertaining to their area. Last time it was the couple who stole cats from the SPCA, took them to the lake, and drowned them.

•

KRISTOF HAD MOVED THE CHEROKEE into the garage. Across the street, Mrs. Strohmeyer was walking her dachsund. Nadia waved, smiled. The dog was curling its hot-dog back, laying its hot-dog turds. It could be worse, Nadia imagined saying to Peter on the phone. He could be a serial dog killer. One of those people who leave hamburger balls mixed with ground glass in the park.

Sure. He could be the Unabomber. He could be the Vampire of Bytów.

She opened the front door. Smelled flowers and garlic. "Kristof!" she called.

"Hey, Mom," he called from the kitchen. "Shit!"

"Drop something?"

"Shrimp marengo. Damn things slip. Do you *have* to devein?"

"I don't know." Nadia set down her purse. Still in their wrapping the flowers lay, begging for water, on the dining room table. Tulips and baby's breath. "I'm allergic to shrimp. You know that."

"No shit!" He appeared in the doorway of the kitchen, his T-shirt spotted with shrimp leavings, a paring knife in one hand. "How much is a clove of garlic?"

"They vary. One of those big pieces is a good-sized clove. Or you could use two smaller ones."

"You're kidding! I thought it was the whole—you know, the whole *thing*."

112

"A bulb has about ten cloves in it."

"Fuck! No wonder it all stinks!"

He raced back to the kitchen. Nadia sat on the carpeted stairs and removed her shoes, which pinched. She had always been allergic to shrimp. When Peter still lived with them, she sometimes served battered shrimp for the four of them and a hamburger for herself. She'd sigh and say, "Wow, that looks good. But Mama's allergic."

Pushing herself up, she padded into the dining room, found a vase in the bottom cupboard, filled it at the kitchen sink.

"What's *that* for?" said Kristof.

Nadia nodded at the flowers.

"Shit!" he said. "They're wrecked."

"They are fine," Nadia said. She reached out to touch Kristof's elbow, which was batting like a chicken wing, working the shrimp. "What is not fine," she said in Polish, as he shrugged her off, "is being off your meds."

When she had arranged the tulips, she left him alone. Upstairs, in the bathroom, sat the translucent orange bottles, the complicated lids with tabs like tongues. Once, years back, Kristof had thrown a full bottle to the floor and stomped on it with his boots. Amber flew everywhere; the pills ground to pink powder. For weeks after, she ran across needle-shaped plastic shards, under the toilet, caught between tile and grout.

This time, sitting on her bed, she spilled the caplets out and counted. Of the Depakote, twenty-five left. Last week there had been forty. Kristof was supposed to take four a day. The Lampresal was down by fourteen; two a day. They were fine on the Lampresal. Just the stabilizer not taken. He was a table with a broken leg.

She called Kristof's shrink, Dr. Horvath, a worried guy whom Kristof barely tolerated. "Doctor's service," came an impatient voice.

"Is he available?" Nadia asked.

"He'll be picking up messages. If this is an emergency, he can be paged."

Nadia pushed the pills around on her bedside table "Ask him to call," she said.

They were hard to spot, the emergencies. There had been weeks when Kristof did nothing but sleep, for instance. And weeks when he had not slept, it seemed, a wink. There was the stash of yard-sale clock radios in the basement, Kristof down there trying out each one's whine or buzz or click. "Are you going to sell them?" Nadia asked once.

He stared at her. "I have to *fix* them first," he said. And trundled out to buy more.

There had been the night he grabbed two pool cues and swished them through the air in front of Nadia's face, like Bruce Lee with his chains. In high school there had been the money that disappeared from her wallet, and the sudden appearance of lacrosse equipment. Kristof didn't play lacrosse. The night he bound and gagged Lili—now there was an emergency. Nadia and Peter had gone out to dinner and left Hanna in charge and Hanna had fallen asleep and Kristof had swaddled Lili and left her with the spiders by the furnace.

Peter had taken Lili, after that one, and gone to Baltimore.

The rest you couldn't call emergencies. Not the Egypt mania that had seized him in sixth grade, when he wallpapered his room in hieroglyphics and sculpted a life-sized Isis from construction foam. Certainly not Kristof's other homemade meals, pizza spilling onto the oven floor or chicken curry thickened with a whole box of cornstarch. Your papa had episodes, Nadia's mother had said when she was still alive. Bad enough for me to leave him in Kraków and come here. But not so bad as this one.

When the doorbell rang, Nadia jumped—as if, for a moment, there had been the possibility of that ponytailed couple standing there with their banner. Detecting guilt, they had followed her home.

"Kristof!" she called. She dribbled the pills back into their jar. A thump from the kitchen. Kristof was dropping things. Lili was away at college, safe; Hanna had moved to Florida. Stumbling to the bathroom, Nadia drenched a blue washcloth with cold water, pressed it to her face, patted dry, descended. At the door, pierced like an earring board, stood Kristof's girl-friend, Lori.

"Hey, Nadia. Kristof in?"

"Can you not smell him?" said Nadia.

Lori sniffed. She was a perky, pretty girl, despite some residual acne damage to her chin and lower cheeks. When she actually got her dentistry degree, she said, she was going to take the piercings out. They would frighten patients too much; would remind them of pain. Now she clacked her tongue stud against her lower teeth. "They say garlic cures a cold," she said. "Hey, Kristo-boy!"

"God! You have got to help me!" Kristof called from the kitchen. Lori winked at Nadia. Lori thought Kristof was a clown. I know, I know, she'd said when Nadia tried to tell her about the darker side. I just wait it out. He doesn't mean a bit of it.

"I'll let you two be," said Nadia.

"Nonsense! Mom! I made this for you!"

In the kitchen, Kristof twirled. He offered a shrimp by its tail and Lori bit off the body. A handsome boy, though not as tall as his long-lost Polish father. On the Risperdal he'd gained twenty pounds in three months. Now he was back to his wiry self, a sprite dancing around his queen. Nadia lifted the pot lid from the rice, breathed its plain scent.

"I wanted to do crème brulée for dessert," Kristof said, "but I got too involved with deveining."

"That's important," said Lori. "Those veins are really the shrimp's intestine. They can be full of gross stuff."

She dipped a spoon into the sauce and tasted it. "That'll cure a cold," she said.

"Will it make you pregnant?" Kristof asked.

"Kristof!" Lori twisted out of his arm. "Do you *want* me pregnant?" she said. Her blue eyes showed just the trace of alarm.

"Might be fun. Hey, you and my mom can both be pregnant. Sit around and knit booties together."

He leered at Nadia, or rather in Nadia's direction. His eyes focused somewhere to the left of Nadia's waist. Nadia held her breath.

"Well, I don't want to be pregnant," said Lori, trying to steer back to the land of light banter. "Not until I've set up a practice."

"Good girl," said Nadia.

"Well, then"—Kristof set a can of olives on the counter and fished around for the opener—"my mom will have to go through her confinement alone."

Lori glanced at Nadia. "I am not pregnant," said Nadia.

Suddenly she knew why Kristof had gone off his meds. Anger rose in her like steam.

"Really?" said Kristof. "I am sorry to hear that, Mom. It's not for lack of trying," he said as an audible aside to Lori.

Lori brightened. "You're dating?" she asked Nadia.

Nadia made fists, released them. "I would hardly call it that," she said.

"Well, don't be Oedipal, boyfriend!" said Lori. She took a kitchen towel and flicked Kristof lightly on the back with it.

"I'm not!" protested Kristof. "I just don't think fifty-year-old babes ought to be sneaking around. Doing the hotel scene." He dumped the olives into the simmering shrimp before Nadia had a chance to suggest draining them.

"What makes you think," she asked her son, insisting now on Polish, forcing a smile to stay on her face, "I do the hotel scene?"

"Clerk called four days ago," said Kristof. "Said you'd left some personal things."

Four days ago. Perfect.

"Well, if they were personal," said Lori, ready to mediate, "then they are your mom's business. Hey, we are all grown-ups here!"

"Absolutely," said Kristof. He lifted the skillet, swimming in shrimp, and carried it out to the dining room. "Consequences happen, though. Especially if you forget your personal things."

"Oh, please," said Lori, following him with the rice. She rolled her eyes in Nadia's direction.

The facts were these. After Peter left, there had been two men, one Polish, one American, the Pole during the year Kristof had been off trying to cope with college. They had both pulled away once they saw what a handful Nadia's son was. This town didn't offer much. You went through a second husband and two lovers, and you were at the bottom of the barrel. For the last few months, Nadia had been hanging around one of the hotel bars after work. She was no longer young, but neither was anyone else. Once or twice—no, three or four times—she had taken a room. The men were married, of course. But they weren't around enough to back away from her son. She didn't have to hear them say, as if to a condemned person, "I am so sorry, Nadia."

"So I'm driving over this way," said Lori brightly when they were seated. She had already begun separating out the chunks of garlic. Nadia had served herself rice with butter and a few tomato chunks. "And they are holding a vigil, can you believe it? For that poor little pooch."

"You heard about that, huh?" said Kristof. He scooped shrimp and rice into his mouth.

"Who hasn't heard about it? You know my mom keeps Pomeranians. She says they are the *smartest* dogs." Lori said this to Nadia, who nodded as if she were in the market for a canine. "And my sister knows that Melinda Mayhew."

Kristof had swallowed, made a bellows of his cheeks, and blown. "Whew!" he said. "That's some garlic bulb!"

"My sister sells Mary Kay to her. She says that lady won't stop till she finds the guy. My sister says she's nuts."

"I'll second that," said Kristof.

Nadia let her jaw drop. *No no no*, she sent the message to her son. He was pouring more wine, warm Chardonnay he'd found in the cabinet. He wasn't supposed to drink alcohol. But you picked your battles, and meds were in the field. *No no no don't tell her!*

"You know her?" said Lori. She tugged at her eyebrow ring. "Is that a coincidence or what, Nadia? Kristof knows that poor lady, too! And she really is nuts? I've always hated Poms myself. Little panters."

Kristof started giggling. He spat a couple of masticated shrimp onto his plate and couldn't stop. He pounded the table with his fist. His eyes teared. "I'm sorry. I am *sorry*," he said when he'd gained an ounce of control. The giggles still sprung from him, like hiccups. He drained his glass of wine. "But it was just so *funny*. *God* you should've seen. Like one of those stunts in the movies, when the pet goes hurling across the screen. Like, where'd the *brakes* go? Jesus." He wiped his eyes. "It was a satisfying moment. And yes, Lori, she is nuts."

"What are you talking about?" said Lori. She pulled at the studs that dotted her ear cartilage. "What was so funny? Stop *choking*. Lordy."

"Little poochie." He thrust his arms in front of him, the hands fisted to make paws. "Aaah!"

"You're the—you're the guy?" Lori paused with her wine glass halfway to her lips. "The guy in the red truck? Who hit that poor lady? And threw away her *dog*?"

"*She* hit *me*, A. B, you just said she was not that poor lady but that nuts lady. C, guilty."

Lori's arm refused to move. Her elbow stayed in a precise V. All that past winter, when Kristof had been paralyzed with depression, she had stuck it out. Had gone to Dr. Horvath to learn what she could do. Kristof had told her she made him want to puke and still she had stuck it out. Once you know how sweet he can be, she had said to Nadia, you can't give up on him.

Now she rose, her wine barely wavering in the glass. "The awful thing," she said, "is that I believe you."

"That's me. *Nyilt* Kristof, honest Kris."

"Someone ought to call the police." Lori's tongue stud clacked. She looked to Nadia, who moved her shrimp around her plate.

"Go ahead," said Kristof.

Lori set her wine down on the table, turned, and walked out. "Good luck, Nadia," she called over her shoulder, sounding eerily like Peter.

•

NEXT DAY NADIA FOUND HERSELF at the Beau Repos cemetery, where she laid eyes on Melinda Mayhew.

All day, again, the incident had been on the news, a tragicomic punctuation to world events. The drivers of the oncoming cars were interviewed. "I thought it was a T-shirt flying through the air," said one young woman; another said, "People on our side of the road were very friendly. The fellow whose wheels went over him, he was very upset." At work, Nadia's colleagues talked about tailgaters, pork-barrel road construction projects, and some people's obsession with bringing their pets on car rides. After work, Nadia had simply headed toward the plaza by the expressway. The ceremony was in progress when she arrived. A black-robed minister officiated, and people were bowing their heads. All around them were little stone markers, for Fluffy and Terrence and Beauregard, "our faithful one." The ponytailed lady stood next to the minister. Spotting Nadia, she wiggled fingers at her, a new friend. Nadia nodded briefly, then bowed her head with the rest.

"Those who are faithful to us unto the end," the minister intoned, "those who connect us with the mystery of God's whole creation, those who place their trust in us, their sacred trust. What can we say but that Samantha gave her life for her mistress?"

Nadia cried. Granted, she cried easily on such occasions. This time she thought of the Lab, the spaniel, the terrier. If Kristof ever left home, she would get dogs again. She would be one of those old women who lived for their dogs. At this she cried.

"I would not be surprised," said a voice at her ear when the service concluded, "if the guilty party were among those present. Would you?"

It was Dean Dexter, the photographer. "What makes you think that?" said Nadia, wiping her eyes.

"It's too strange a crime to be as random as it appears. Killing a person's pet is a crime of passion, a revenge crime. Who has something against Ms. Mayhew?"

He nodded in the direction of a tall, athletic-looking woman who stood by the minister in a posture of embarrassment and anger. The others present had started to murmur, to break up and drift off.

"Excuse me," said Nadia. She stepped over to the tall woman, almost tripping on a hidden headstone. "Miss Mayhew?"

"Call me Mel," said the woman. Her voice was gravelly, a smoker's voice.

"What a tragedy for you," said Nadia.

"A dead child is a tragedy. A dead dog is sad and weird."

Mel Mayhew wore a business suit and sneakers. Behind her, the expressway whined. "Samantha was my mom's dog," she went on. "I promised Mom I'd take care of her when Mom died." She kicked a clump of grass with her sneakered foot. "The rest is just stupid," she said. She looked over Nadia's shoulder. "Can you get that guy out of here?" she asked.

Nadia turned. At her back, Dean Dexter was scribbling notes. "*Na litosc boska*," Nadia said. "For heaven's sake."

"News is news," he said.

"Try 'Girl hits boy,'" said Nadia.

"You know something, don't you?"

She looked closely at him. He was fifty, or almost. No wedding ring. Somewhere behind his inquisitive eyes, a failed passion. The joy she would bring him, telling him about Kristof, was hideous to contemplate. "I know," she said slowly, "how complicated the world is."

•

120

SHE'D KEPT HER PHONE OFF during the ceremony and missed a call from Dr. Horvath. She came home to Kristof still asleep—amazing how deeply he could sleep, like a patient etherized. The Mr. Coffee had turned to sludge. Two messages on the machine. The first was from Lili, giggling, could Mom send her those green slippers, the ones she wore on visits? The second was Lori, who knew Kristof didn't use his cell anymore for fear of radiation. Lori was crying. She was going to call the police. "Even though I do hate Poms," she said, snuffling. "You could gun down a hundred Poms as far as I'm concerned. Make coats out of their fur. Only they mustn't *belong* to somebody, Kristof. It's—it's the love thing. Whatever people love. It's not up to you to take it away."

She had called, she said, to give Kristof time. In case he wanted to leave town. She would call the police in a half hour, she said. She knew Kristof was home. She'd driven by and peeked in the window of the garage at the Cherokee.

Nadia slipped off her shoes. She went upstairs. "Kristof, *lelkem*, honey," she said, shaking his shoulder. The odor he gave off was ripe, a man's odor. "You need to get up," she said.

"Right," he said, and turned away from her.

"The police are on their way. Lori called them. And Dr. Horvath called."

He did not stir. Nadia sighed, then went to the bathroom. This was Peter's technique. She filled the bathroom cup with water, returned to Kristof's room, and said, "Now, Kristof." When he only mumbled, she tipped the cup. Water trickled onto his neck.

"Goddamnit!" he said. Nadia stepped back when he jumped from the bed. It was, she used to tell Peter, the worst way to wake a person up. The most effective, too, he said. "Mom," Kristof said, hulking over her, his lips tight and his eyes narrowed, "I am *asleep*."

"Not now, you're not," she said. She took his elbow and steered him downstairs. "Listen to this," she said. As she flicked on the answering machine, the doorbell rang.

•

THE DETECTIVE, A YOUNG, GOOD-NATURED MAN with a badge reading "Connolly," began gently. They had had a report, Connolly said. Their duty was to investigate. Could they speak—?

Kristof wouldn't give. "I was just joking. Jeez," he said when Nadia let the cop in. His eyes, awake now, danced at his mother. "You take everything so *seriously*."

"Kristof, please," Nadia said.

Connolly wrote things down on a little pad. He'd already been out back, to have a gander at the red truck. He looked around the front hallway as if he could find a clue in the corners of the ceiling. "I could take you down to the station now," he said to Kristof, "or you could come on down yourself. Any time tonight."

Nadia waited for Kristof to answer, then said, "Which is better?"

"I'd follow us down, if I was you. Make it easier. After twelve hours I'll have to send someone out here."

"I guess we'll stop by later," said Nadia. She put her hand on Kristof's shoulder. If the police would just leave—another squad car sat at the curb, now, and a couple of unknown cars had parked across the street—she would page Dr. Horvath. Kristof is aiming for residential treatment by court order, Horvath would say; let him get what he's after. Still. "Just give us a couple hours," she said.

"No pressure," said Connolly. He took her hand. His palm was warm and dry, his fingers thick. She wanted to keep hold of his hand, but he squeezed and then pulled away and reached for Kristof's, which didn't come out of Kristof's pants pocket.

The door closed behind Connolly. The house still smelled, faintly, of shrimp. Already it was evening, a Friday, the time of week when people like Nadia gathered at the hotel bar and recapped their restless week. "Poor cop," Kristof was saying. "He does this shit for a living."

"Honey, get dressed," said Nadia. "We're going down there."

"I got other places to go," said Kristof.

He laid his hand on the railing and skipped steps, vaulting up. Nadia waited for the slam of his bedroom door, the rattling of his dresser drawer. Some days he shoved the clothes in, and when they stuck in the hinges he yanked the drawers open. Other days—rare ones—he had taken everything out and folded it beautifully, and the shirts and pants were stacked in triple rows worthy of Wally Cleaver.

She crossed her arms in the hallway. She would call Horvath. If he came over, they might persuade Kristof down to the station, and from there maybe to signing himself in for treatment. Just to get the meds back in sync. The door squeaked, overhead. Only it wasn't Kristof's. Nadia's eyes snapped open.

By the time she reached the landing, Kristof's feet were disappearing up the attic ladder.

"*Lelkem?*" said Nadia. "Kristof?"

Gingerly she set her bare feet on the metal rungs. Unfinished planks on the attic floor covered the fiber insulation; here and there sat Have-a-Heart traps that they had used in the spring to catch squirrels. Nothing was stored in the attic. There was only one reason anyone—Kristof—went up here. At the far end, behind the chimney, he had shrugged off his slippers. Waning daylight angled through the trap door to the roof. "Kristof?" Nadia said again; but with the trap dislodged, he had hoisted himself up.

"*Srać,*" she swore. She stood on the planks, straightened, and thunked her head on a beam. "*Srać!* Shit!" She bent; she scuttled, crablike. The last time he had pulled this stunt had been the weekend before Peter left, and she had stood on a frozen lawn and shouted up at him, had pleaded, had talked him down.

This time she reached her arms through the opening to the roof and tried to hoist herself up and through, as her son had done. But the arms were too weak, the body too heavy. "Goddammit, Kristof!" she called. She heard his steps, moving over

123

the roof tiles. The roof slanted, but at a shallow pitch. "Pull me up!" she demanded. Her voice sounded small, in the muffled space of the attic. His feet stopped moving.

Nadia pulled over one of the Have-a-Heart traps. How long had it been since they trapped a squirrel? And driven it out of the city, far into the hills, to set it free in the woods where it could tell its new clan about the wonders of town life. Kristof had loved those trips, Lili too. Nadia dragged over the other trap, stacked it, stepped carefully onto the flimsy cages, and pulled herself out to the roof.

"Mom," Kristof said without turning. "You made it."

"Don't scare me, Kristof," she said. She stood and squinted against the setting sun. Her son was a silhouette farther down on the slope of the roof, facing west.

"No fear," he said.

He lifted his arms, like wings. Nadia's throat bulged closed. From below, in the gathering darkness, came a scream. Carefully she took two steps forward. The rough tiles held her feet. Below, cars lined their street. Their passengers were getting out. Nadia counted. The fourth in was a white Mazda: Melinda Mayhew. A couple of cars behind her, the ponytailed couple's van. Then from beside the first, rusty blue car came a flash, and Dean Dexter called out, "You okay up there?"

"We're fine," Nadia said. Only softly, not to him; to Kristof. You didn't make something happen by shouting. "Back up a step, *lelkem*," she said.

"I like it here."

The open air flattened his voice. Nadia inched forward, the grip of the tiles a sure thing. Reaching up, she took her son's outstretched hand. It was a big hand, a man's hand. She managed just to wrap her fingers around the palm. The sun slipped below the tops of the trees. As the breeze brought a far-off wail, they blessed the multitudes.

Sunset District

IT WASN'T ABOUT THE DOG.

Mimi lay awake listening for her daughter Jean to return from walking what Jean insisted on calling a German shepherd. Collie, that dog had in it, and a trace of Staffordshire terrier. But Mimi hadn't argued. Jean's husband, Marc, had wanted a German shepherd for his birthday, and Jean—doing her best to please—had found something advertised on Craigslist, pure-bred but no papers. Mimi wasn't about to point out what was fishy. The point was that Jean loved her peculiar husband. Love, Mimi tried to tell herself, was a good thing.

But she had been visiting four days, and she couldn't figure these night walks with the dog. The routine started just before 10 p.m., when she was settled with a Scotch and Jean with a cup of herb tea and they were talking. It was the chief joy of having grown children, Mimi thought—this conversation late at night in the grown daughter or son's place (Mimi, widowed now, had two of each), where anything at all could come up. Mimi had no strings attached to her children. They all supported themselves. Jean was in graduate school, but a state school, and she worked in the registrar's office; Marc, whom she'd married two years ago, had a trust fund. Mimi wasn't inclined to pass judgment on her kids. She enjoyed their company, and they hers. This was especially true of Jean, waifish Jean, who had always been her secret favorite.

But right around 9:55, Jean started glancing at her watch, and within a few minutes, no matter how much tea remained in the mug or interest in the conversation, she announced she needed to take Boo for a walk. For three nights running, Mimi had picked up a magazine while Jean collected the dog and the leash and the plastic bag. Then, a few minutes after the front door closed, Mimi set the magazine down and drifted into the kitchen to wash the tea mug and clean up the odds and ends. Soon she got herself ready for bed and settled onto the futon that Jean and Marc kept in the second bedroom of their little flat, the one they used as a study. She switched on the cumbersome floor lamp, opened her novel, and read until she could no longer keep her eyes open. At some point in her early sleep she heard Jean tiptoe in; last night, she had kept her eyes shut as Jean entered the room, switched off the lamp, moved the open book from her mother's torso, and kissed her lightly on the forehead in the dark. Mimi had smelled something then that made her uncomfortable. The next morning she woke pondering what the smell was, and what these late-night forays were, because they certainly were not for the sake of the dog.

Marc was not home for Mimi's visit. Both Jean and Mimi pretended this was unfortunate. In fact Marc, at least in Mimi's eyes, had proved a disappointment. At first she had thought him a true catch, a dreamboat, the kind of fellow she would never have thought Jean could land. He was tall, handsome, smart, and monied, and on her first visit to San Francisco, when the two of them were going steady, Mimi had actually flirted with him. When Jean had announced their engagement, it was Mimi who suggested they move up the wedding. "I don't see what you're waiting for," she had said. "You love each other. You want to get married. He has enough money. Get married."

Recently Mimi had begun regretting her advice. This Marc character was not exactly advancing his career. He was a composer, according to Jean—though all he did was manipulate a soundboard and the computer—and he spent most of his time applying for grants. Did Jean understand his music? Mimi had wanted to know. Jean had shaken her head and chuckled, no, Marc played his work for her but she wasn't sophisticated enough. Marc belonged to an electronic collective that

126

performed on the internet. The internet! Mimi was a practical woman. This fellow's trust fund had looked appealing, but it wouldn't support a family. She saw her daughter holding up her share while this dreamy guy let the years float by. Worse, Mimi did not understand why a young man would take off for three months in Indonesia, leaving his wife working and earning money at home.

"He asked me to come," Jean explained, over tea and Scotch. "But I didn't know what I'd do, over there. And we've got Boo."

"His dog," Mimi observed.

"His, yes. Ours." Jean fidgeted on the couch. "I bought Boo."

"And if both of you decided to tour Indonesia," Mimi pointed out, "you'd have no income."

"It's not touring, Mom," Jean insisted. "He's studying the gamelan."

"Can't you study the gamelan in America?"

"Not really, no."

Mimi woke early in the morning—still on East Coast time—and made coffee, then took the dog for its morning run. It was something she could do, she had told Jean. Jean had never liked dogs, especially large ones. She had been frightened of them as a kid—such a spindly, skittish child she had been—and had actually been bitten by one on a camping trip. She still bore the scar, a wavery white line in her right cheek, just above her jaw. That she had found this supposed German shepherd and brought it into her life for Marc's sake said either that she loved the guy very much or that she thought she was losing him. In any case, Mimi thought it was good to get the dog onto the beach, let it run off its energy and not jump up on her girl so much. She was sure that, whatever Jean did with the dog in the late evening, she did not run it on the moonlit beach.

Gripping the retractable leash, she let Boo haul her the dozen blocks to the ocean. Outside was gray, the commercial buildings on Taraval Street various shades of beige, the whole thing like a washed-out color snapshot from the early Sixties.

She had not expected San Francisco to be so dreary. This district was called the Sunset, Jean had told her; it was the place Mark Twain had been referring to when he said the coldest winter he'd ever spent was a summer in San Francisco. The east-west streets followed the alphabet as they proceeded southward; Taraval lay between Santiago and Ulloa. The state university, where Jean attended her psychology classes and worked, was just past Yorba and up one of the hills that kept the low clouds and the fog hovering over the Sunset.

Mimi passed through the tunnel under the highway that ran along the coast and emerged onto the wide, windswept beach, where the ocean thundered in. A low mist hung over the sand. Yesterday, there had been a group of men here in the early morning, performing stunts with surfboards and a kite-like contraption they strapped to their backs. They rode the waves, then lifted off into the air and tried to land on the crest of the water. They had all worn wet suits, the water being so frigid, and one who was strapping himself up had told Mimi there was a terrible rip tide here, and no one ever really went swimming. He had been shockingly middle-aged, this man. Mimi wondered why he was still risking his life this way and whether he didn't have something better to do on a Wednesday morning; but then, when he flew through the air, she laughed aloud and admired his bravado. Now she glanced around for any people before she let the dog off the leash. While Boo chased a group of seagulls, she slipped off her flats and dug her toes into the harsh, cold sand.

It was not a pretty place, she told herself, where Jean lived. The ocean was strange and wild, but not beautiful with the coast highway whizzing by. The flat itself was nice enough, but the neighborhood desultory and the beach littered with ciga-rette butts and plastic bottles and old newspapers. What had that smell been, last night? Mimi breathed the salt air, its rank odors of seaweed and fish. Sex, she thought. That's what it had been. The smell of sex. Jean had taken the dog for a walk and had sex with a man. While Marc was in Indonesia, she was having an affair.

The realization sent Mimi to a huge piece of driftwood, where she sat heavily. What an awful secret she suddenly possessed. Jean! A pretty girl, yes, with her narrow nose and fine long neck and graceful collarbone, her slow-spreading smile, and so intelligent, of course—but Jean daring to transgress? Jean grabbing hold, the way the girls did these days, of her sexual desire? Mimi felt her vision getting blurry, as if her eager, cautious daughter stood right in front of her but she couldn't make her out clearly. A breeze had kicked up; she pushed her hair out of her eyes. She had colored it just before she came out—a new color, streaky chestnut brown. Her other daughter, Lacey, told her it made her look young. Jean hadn't said anything. Not because she was unkind, but because she never noticed things like hair, nails, a new handbag. When she was Mimi's age, Mimi predicted, her lovely, milky-skinned daughter would look like a stringy-haired hag. She herself would be long gone by then; still, it bothered her sometimes, that she should put a better face toward the world than Jean did. But now what was Jean doing, with her husband out of town? Seeing a man. What man, and why would she not tell Mimi?

The dog was racing far down the beach, and when Mimi glanced up, she saw a runner, his back to her, jogging north. He must have passed right by and she hadn't noticed; now the dog was at his heels, barking, its heavy long tail swishing.

"Boo!" Mimi cried. "Boo, come here!"

As if responding to her voice, the runner turned and kicked the dog. It was a sudden turn and quite a vicious kick, Mimi could see, even though she was fifty yards away and her glasses fogging up. As she stood, the runner seemed to stare straight at her before he turned away. Did she know the man? Something in his walk—but he wore a baseball cap, shading his face. The dog yelped and staggered back. "Boo!" she cried again, and

129

stumbled over the grass to where the dog stood, its tail still wagging, looking perplexed as the runner loped far away over the sand.

"Oh, honey," she said. She crouched and scratched behind the dog's ears. He was fine, of course—a big healthy young dog. He tried to lick her face, but she straightened up. "Let's get you leashed," she said.

•

JEAN WAS IN THE SHOWER. Mimi wiped the dog's paws, made coffee, toasted a bagel for herself. Jean would be off as soon as she dressed, taking one of those porta-mugs with her to the university. Sitting at the little kitchen table, bright with hazy light, Mimi felt herself trembling. She sipped coffee to steady her nerves. There was something hostile in the air, she thought, here in San Francisco. All those tech companies, turning people cutthroat. The way that man had kicked at the dog, and glanced at her, as if it were all her fault. And then Jean's affair, which she was hiding so effectively in her manner if not in her late-night pattern. Well, why shouldn't she have an affair? This husband of hers was proving unsatisfactory on all counts. They had no children. Though she had remained faithful to her husband, Bill, until cancer took him, Mimi wasn't some kind of judgmental prude about these things. She loved her children; she wanted their happiness. So why didn't Jean tell her about it, about this affair, about wanting to leave her marriage?

Mimi nibbled at her bagel. Keeping quiet: that was the hard thing. Not to just blurt it out that she understood what Jean was up to. Mimi tended to speak her mind. She believed in speaking her mind. It was what she had done when Jean first announced that she was engaged. Same with Jean's sister, Lacey. In Lacey's case, Mimi had expressed her strong feeling that Lacey should not marry Paul, who had been her only boyfriend in college. Not that Mimi had had anything against Paul. She only thought Lacey should live a little, see something of the world, know what she was getting into. Lacey had told her to

130

stuff it and had married Paul, and now they had the twins. Was Mimi hurt? Not at all. Nor would she had been hurt if Jean had kept her engagement as long as originally planned—two years, she had said—though Mimi's firm opinion was that Jean should put a lock on it while she had the dreamboat interested. Well, it wasn't as if Jean had had the smoothest time of things, was it? Flitting from one school to another, from one guy to another, always so susceptible to what others wanted of her, never confident in her looks or charm the way her sister was. Admit it, Mimi lectured herself, taking another bite of the bagel, so weak. Jean was weak. She needed a protector. That was what Mimi had been thinking, and if Jean had been thinking something else—like, I don't really love Marc—she could have told her mother to stuff it, just as her sister had done.

At a soft kiss on the crown of her head, Mimi almost jumped from her chair. "Thanks for taking Boo," Jean said. Her smile was huge, her damp hair pulled into a thin braid at the nape of her neck.

"You sneaked up on me!"

"I said your name three times, Ma."

Mimi rose quickly, as if she had been caught in the act—of what? Of thinking? "Let me whip up breakfast," she said.

"You've eaten. And I'm late for class." Jean pressed 20 seconds on the microwave; she liked to steam milk for her tea. "I may pack some caffeine this time."

"You look as if you'll need it," Mimi said.

Jean looked sharply at her. The damp air out here was perfect, Mimi had to admit, for her daughter's skin; Jean's complexion was smooth as cream, the freckles like pink sugar sprinkled over her nose. Mimi had read somewhere that the forward focus of the eyes signified that humans were meant to be predators, but Jean's seemed to rebut that idea—not because she was wall-eyed, oh no, but her large, wide-spaced eyes, a pale indeterminate color even with her contacts in, had no prey in mind. "I'm fine," she said, clipping the words.

"You couldn't have gotten much sleep. How late did you get back?"

Jean shrugged. "I don't know. You don't have to walk Boo in the mornings, Ma, if you don't want. I mean, it is pretty late when I get him out. He can just go in the garden and pee."

"But where do you"—Mimi adjusted mid-course—"Why do you walk him such a long time, at night?"

"I just do." Jean laughed nervously. The microwave dinged. She turned to pull out the mug; pouring coffee into it, she spilled some on the counter. "Don't you feel safe here, Ma? This neighborhood's not the best but there's no crime—"

"Some man kicked the dog on the beach this morning."

Jean snapped the lid on. "What do you mean, some man?"

"A runner. He was far down the beach, I didn't see him. Boo ran after him as if"—she tried to recollect; it had happened so fast—"as if he knew him. Wagging his tail. He wasn't getting in the guy's stride or threatening him or anything."

Jean was moving, brushing past her mother, gathering her jacket, her pocketbook. "You probably shouldn't let him off the leash, Ma. He doesn't know you that well. He could run up onto the highway—"

"He knows me perfectly well. If you can't run a dog on the beach, I don't see why—" Mimi stopped herself. She could hear the tone of her own voice rising, launching into argument mode. "I'm just saying," she said as she trailed Jean to the front door, "there was a hostile character on the beach, and there could be hostile characters roaming around after midnight. I know it's a sleepy part of the city here, but—"

"I was back at midnight, Ma," Jean said. She tried to smile, but the effort showed. "I checked my watch."

•

THAT EVENING, JEAN DIDN'T GO OUT. She said they could just let Boo pee in the garden; he hadn't been pooping at night since Mimi had got him in the habit of a long morning run. Mimi had roasted a chicken, which she watched her daughter

132

consume with guilty gluttony. Marc, Jean had confided, had declared himself a vegan six months before, and since she knew he was basically right about all that, she had adjusted her cooking. "Doesn't Marc cook?" Mimi asked, serving her a second thigh.

"He pays for everything when we go out. He likes to go out. Says it makes him feel calm. I guess his parents quarreled a lot at home. In restaurants they had to behave."

"So how often do you go out?"

"I don't know. Two, three times a week?"

Mimi stifled the urge to point out that three restaurant meals a week were not within Marc's budget, trust fund or no trust fund. Instead she said, "And you go to vegetarian restaurants?"

Jean licked her fingers before wiping them on her napkin. A little grease coated her chin. She looked like a happy child. "That's what's funny," she said. "When we go out, Marc eats, like, filet mignon. He says they'll just throw it away otherwise. But I don't order it. He says I'm his conscience."

"You must—you must miss him," Mimi said hesitantly. "It's been, what? A week now?"

Jean took a slow sip of wine. She did not look at her mother. Definitely an affair, Mimi thought. She willed her daughter to tell her. Good, she would say. Just what you need! "I kind of like the time apart, actually," Jean said at last. "Marc can be a little, you know. High maintenance. This way I focus on my work. And he's—he's—" She swung her large eyes around to meet her mother's. "He's happy."

"And that's what matters?"

"Of course that's what matters."

They cleaned up and watched a movie, a "viciously funny" independent production about a self-mutilating young woman and her loathsome boss. "Is that what you're working on?" Mimi asked as the credits rolled and Jean sat hugging her knees. "Girls with issues like that?"

"I'm working on grief, Ma." Jean swiped at her eyes with the back of her palm. "I want to work with people in the grieving process. I told you."

She had not, Mimi was sure, told her. But the movie, however humorous its intent, had obviously upset Jean. Mimi remembered that one incident, when Jean was twelve and Lacey fifteen and Lacey had put her cigarette out on Jean's thigh and Jean had said she told her to. Now, they talked only about the actors and the lame jokes and then about Jean's boss, the chair of the psych department, who was not loathsome at all but chubby and funny according to Jean. Was that the man she was seeing? A chubby joker to replace the filet-eating vegan?

Together they walked Boo, up to the parkway that ran through the Sunset district and down as far as the lake. The sky was clear for once, the moon a bright waxing crescent. Later, as she fell asleep, Mimi heard her daughter's voice from the living room, speaking softly into her cell phone. But at least she hadn't gone out, and Mimi slept more deeply than she had since arriving on the West Coast. When she woke—it was Saturday, her last full day—Jean was already bustling around the kitchen, making French toast. "Hey, sleepyhead," she greeted her mother.

"I'll be hopeless when I get back East," Mimi said.

"I'm sure you'll adjust. You're very adjustable." Jean beamed at her. What was that supposed to mean, adjustable? "I thought we'd go for a drive," Jean went on. "For your last day. Get you out of the Sunset. We could go across the bridge over to Sausalito, take a boat to Angel Island maybe."

"Is that something you'd like to do?"

"Marc and I go all the time. The sun's always shining, on that side of the bay." Jean slid three slices of French toast onto a plate already piled high and tucked it into the oven. Mimi poured coffee from the pot Jean had made for her; Jean herself drank tea, of which there were about two dozen flavors stacked in the cupboard.

"What else do you like to do together?"

Jean shrugged. She was wearing an oversized T-shirt and jeans, and glasses that made her eyes look even larger. "Lots of things," she said. "Last month we went hiking in Yosemite. Sometimes we go to the bookstores in Berkeley. We do brunch at the Cliff House sometimes. We walk Boo all the way up the beach and tie him up, and I bring him a piece of omelette when we're done."

"You go with friends?"

"Oh, no." Jean had microwaved the syrup and now set it on the table. She caught her mother's eye. "Marc doesn't like friends," she said, as if this were a little joke.

"Don't be silly. You always had friends."

"Well, I don't now. I mean, people I work with. People in my classes. But otherwise it's Marc and me."

They had settled at the table. Mimi took two slices of the toast and poured syrup, aware how pleased Jean was to be providing this meal. She reminded herself they had the whole day. No need to press her daughter. Get her to open up a little. Bit by bit it would come out. Who she was seeing, and why, and what her options were now. Mimi felt her senses go on high alert, like an owl in a dark woods. "Do you two get along that way?"

"Did you and Dad?"

"We had friends."

Jean sipped her orange juice. She contemplated her mother—a look, Mimi thought, like a very wise old woman's as she considers the basic ignorance of her audience. "He's got the collective," she said. "It's hard to measure up."

"What do you mean, measure up? Who is he to measure you? What kind of standard—"

"Mom, please." Jean rose; the kettle was whistling. "I shouldn't have said anything. I knew you'd react this way."

"I'm sorry. Let's back up. Who's in this collective? Do *they* make any money?"

"It's like there's…" Jean returned to the table, stirring her

135

tea. She kept her eyes averted, but Mimi could tell from the tightness of her voice that she was close to tears. "There's a kind of blankness," she said, "at Marc's center. The collective fills it. You know, with music."

What they call music, Mimi thought.

"And I don't really."

"What rubbish."

"I don't know if it's rubbish or not. I just know I don't feel—well, *worthy*. So it's kind of a relief to have him gone for a little while."

"And to have"—Mimi lingered over the square of French toast she had cut, the dark syrup glistening—"someone else around?"

"Oh, I like having you around, Ma. This isn't about that."

"I didn't mean me." Mimi ate the square, sipped her coffee. She waited for her daughter to look at her. When she did, Mimi saw it was too late; Jean's face, white from holding back tears, had closed off. Behind the glasses, her eyes were stubborn. They were not going to talk about wherever it was that she went, with the dog, at night. "I just wonder if you should have rushed to marry Marc. If someone else wouldn't have made you happier."

"Rushed!" Suddenly Jean cackled, shrill and artificial. "Who rushed me, Ma? Who never gave me a chance to think twice?"

Mimi put her hand over her heart. "You're not saying that I—"

"'He's got a trust fund, he's comfortable, you love him.' Who said all that?" Jean removed her glasses and wiped them brusquely with a paper napkin. "And again you said it, when I said I was postponing. 'He's got a trust fund. He's got money. Who else are you going to get to love you?'"

"I never said such a thing!"

"Not in those words, no. But over and over you kept asking me why I was waiting. What am I supposed to tell you, Ma? I'm waiting because I think marriage will swallow me whole?"

"Yes, exactly. That's just what you say, darling, if that's what you feel."

"Not to you, Ma. I don't say stuff like that to you." Jean had stood up. Taking the plate of untouched French toast, she opened a drawer and pulled out a roll of plastic wrap. Tomorrow, Mimi thought, she'll zap a slice or two and eat it alone, here in this kitchen. Or will she share it with this new man, whoever he is? "Nothing I could have said," Jean went on, snapping off a length of clear wrap, "would have made sense to you. You're always right about everything. You and Lacey."

"Lacey told you to marry Marc?"

"She told me how you tried to stop her, with Paul. So when she said stuff like 'Follow your heart,' it was like she thought my heart had just one way to go, and that was down the aisle."

"But if you're not happy—"

"No, no. I'll be happy enough. It'll be fine. I just needed a little break, was all. Maybe Marc needed one, too. Let's not talk about it anymore, okay, Ma?"

Jean stepped over and gave the back of Mimi's neck a squeeze, as if Mimi needed bucking up. But Mimi couldn't help noticing the future tense. *I will be happy. It will be fine.* Meaning it wasn't fine now. All through the day, as they drove over the magnificent bridge and walked along the pier at Sausalito and took the little ferry to the island, the sun out and the warm breeze lifting their hair, she tried to think back; to recreate what she had done to her daughter. She did not like this man, this Marc, this so-called composer with his bullying ways. It could not be true that she had forced Jean to marry him. Jean was unhappy and having an affair. She wanted to place the blame for her actions elsewhere, and what handier place than your mother?

Several young men boarded the boat for Angel Island—a trio in baseball caps and two others with their wives or girlfriends. Mimi watched them, watched how they looked at Jean. Quickly they approved of her slender legs, the shorts she wore belted loosely on her hips, her wide but delicately crafted shoulders. Then their eyes went to her face, which was pretty only in an offbeat, hidden way—the mouth a little wide, the chin a little sharp, the scar a white sickle on her cheek, and those doe-like eyes. She looked more fragile than she was, Mimi thought, and only someone who was interested either in taking care of her or breaking her would draw close. The young men's eyes flicked away; they went back to their friends, their own women.

Jean, in the open air, seemed to have let the morning's argument go. "I love this view of the Bay," she said as they shared a bench by the old military buildings on the island. "Sometimes I think, if I ever manage to finish this stupid degree—"

"You're almost done, aren't you? After this year?"

"I have to write a dissertation, remember? And I might need to work full time."

Mimi frowned. "Don't you think it's time for Marc—"

"Please, Ma. Let's not start on Marc again."

Mimi nodded. She wouldn't start. You're so goddamn impatient, Bill used to say, the one fault he found in her. Well, she'd been patient with cancer. She could wait this out.

"I was just going to say," Jean went on, "I'd love to have a practice with a view like this. I'd think it would help people caught up in grief. To look out on the world and see how it's always moving, and changing, and beautiful."

Mimi looked. High puffy clouds floated over the Golden Gate, tangerine in the sun. Waves chopped at the steep cliffs of the island. Back toward Sausalito, a half-dozen sails caught the wind, while a massive freighter passed beneath the bridge. Sounds carried across from the shore—a police siren, a ship's bell, shouts. For the first time since arriving in San Francisco, she missed Bill, who would have brought binoculars, would have pinpointed some discovery and then passed them to her. "So they won't miss what they've lost?" she asked.

Jean managed to smile. "You always miss it. Loss is a thing to be managed."

Do you manage? Mimi wanted to ask. The only loss her children had faced, really, had been their dad's death five years ago. Mimi thought they had all come through a bit battered, but with colors flying. Had Jean taken it harder than the others? Was that why she had chosen this graduate program? Maybe that was something they could talk about, Mimi thought, on her last evening. Death and grief, so much easier than love and sex.

But when they had gotten back home and Jean had showered, the evening grew late more suddenly than seemed possible. Mimi fixed her last meal—tetrazzini, with the leftover chicken and wild mushrooms she'd found at the little market down the block—then Jean took a break to check her email while Mimi cleaned up. Once again, just as they settled together on the living room couch, Jean with her tea and Mimi with her Scotch, Jean announced she would walk Boo.

"Why don't we walk him together?" Mimi asked.

"That's okay." Jean was already getting up from the couch, moving toward the kitchen. "You have packing to do."

"All dirty clothes, it'll take five minutes. I liked walking him with you before."

"But this time I'll be walking him a long time."

"But why?" Mimi heard the whine in her voice, but she didn't care. "We walked all day," she said.

"Exactly. I don't want to wear you out." Jean returned from the kitchen, her jacket on. The dog milled around her, wagging its slow tail. She crossed her arms and contemplated her mother. "I want a few minutes alone, okay?"

"I'm leaving first thing tomorrow."

"I know. I know. And we had a great time today, didn't we?" She came over and perched on the arm of the couch. She put her long, cool fingers on Mimi's shoulder. The dog tried to lick her hand, but she pulled it away. "I had a great time," she said. "All this visit."

Mimi didn't want to look up. She didn't want to accuse her

daughter of lying. Instead she regarded the dog. "He's not a pure German shepherd, you know."

"Yeah, Marc pointed that out. He's got collie in him. My bad."

"Do you like having him? You used to be frightened of big dogs."

Jean touched her scar. "Yeah. But he makes Marc happy." She looked at the dog, who had sat back on his haunches, huge mouth agape, ears up, expectant. "Gets me out on walks."

"Sounds like Marc can be pretty persuasive." When Jean didn't answer, Mimi went on, "I found him sort of a flirt, when I first met him."

"What, he flirted with *you*?"

"Yup." Mimi blushed. "Charming the old lady, I guess. He teased me about my voice. Used that old line—was it F. Scott Fitzgerald who said it?—said my voice was full of money." She paused, remembering. "Now I think of it," she said, "it was sort of hostile. The way flirting is sometimes."

Jean bent and scratched the dog's ears. She rose from the armrest. She kissed the top of her mother's head—the same sort of gesture she had given the dog, Mimi thought, assuring both of them that Jean loved them despite their flaws. "It's the same with his music," she observed. "He says every encounter should be a challenge. Come on, Boo."

As soon as the door shut behind her daughter and the dog, Mimi set down her Scotch. She found her sneakers in the spare room. Rummaging quickly in a dresser, she located a dark sweater and pulled it on. From the shelf by the front door she took the key Jean had made for her. Then she followed her daughter out. Challenge my eye, she thought.

Already, Jean and the dog were at the corner, crossing Taraval. Mimi followed on sneakered feet, moving quickly under the streetlamps and pausing whenever she saw the dog pause to sniff or mark. She wished she had worn a dark cap; her hair, with its streaks, caught the light. But Jean did not turn except to tug at the leash. Again and again they crossed the alphabet streets, heading northward—Pacheco, Ortega, Noriega. Mimi began to wonder. Maybe all Jean was doing was walking Boo. Then they reached Judah, and Jean turned left, toward the ocean.

Under a streetlamp, Mimi checked her watch. It had been fifteen minutes—not enough time, even if Jean circled down to the beach and back, to account for the time she was usually gone. Mimi's legs were tired, but she waited until Jean and the dog had cleared the corner, then trotted up to peer down the lit street.

This street was different from most of the others, which had all been residential, row upon row of modest housing, most of the windows dark by now, a few with the blue light of a TV. Like Taraval, Judah had storefronts and even a couple of bars still open. Jean passed a few people walking out from the bars and had to pull the dog away from sniffing. In the third block, Mimi saw the sign before Jean stopped. It was red, the capital letters rounded, the neon not yet burnt out: HOTEL. So she had been right, she thought wildly, sliding around a pair of men arguing on the sidewalk, Jean was meeting a man, was having an affair.

The dog started wagging his tail even before the man stepped out from the shadows. Mimi had drawn dangerously close, but there were people on this street, and she hugged the stucco sides of the buildings. With the sagging pullover and the sneakers, she had to look like a bag lady; not even the drunks had accosted her. The man stepped out, under the streetlamp, and she gasped.

It was Marc. Marc, Jean's husband, who was supposed to be half a world away. But he was here, in the Sunset, leaning down to scratch the dog's head, leaning again to brush Jean's lips with his.

Her eyes ran over his body, the lanky build and easy grace of him. All this time, he had been here. Not in Indonesia, not

141

studying the gamelan. Not conveniently gone, but inconveniently tucked away, just so he would not have to see, to deal with Mimi. Or had Jean tucked him away? *It's all right darling, I'll come to you every night with Boo, I'll manage the old bitch myself.* Staring at her daughter's secret husband, Mimi realized that she had seen him once already this week. On the beach, with Boo—he had been the runner in the fog, he had been the one who delivered that vicious kick. Her stomach hollowed. That he would turn like that, would aim a boot at the belly of the dog his wife had bought just for him—! How he must hate her, this vegan, dog-kicking man, how he must hate his mother-in-law, to do such a thing.

Was she a monster? A hot flush of shame rose into Mimi's face. What a fool she had been, to think herself welcome. All her difficult, honest talk with her daughter that morning had been a lie. Jean was not relieved to have Marc gone, because Marc was not gone. She wanted Mimi to feel awful for having pushed her into this marriage—not because she was ready to leave the marriage, but because it pleased her to make her mother feel awful. Thus did Mimi's favorite behave.

Dizzy with anger and confusion, Mimi backed away, further into the shadows, into the portico of the building to which she had been clinging. Her gaze shifted. Now she saw Jean, her daughter, in the amber light. Jean touched her husband's sleeve. She smiled at him. It was not a genuine smile, but the tense grin that Jean put on when she was hoping to please, hoping to keep everything on an even keel. She was talking softly to him, telling him about her day, assuring him that the old bitch would be gone the next morning—Mimi couldn't hear the words, but their meaning was plain enough. Jean's voice was full not of money but of sweet words and half-truths. If Mimi stepped out of the shadows, now, Jean would say she had gone along with this ridiculous arrangement—walking the dog to the seedy hotel, having sex with Marc, walking home, all the while claiming Marc was an ocean away—not to hurt her mother's feelings. That, too, would be a lie. Jean did not trust her mother. She could not tell her mother of her husband's loathing. She could not admit that she herself would walk the dark streets at night rather than insist that her husband stuff it and welcome her mother. Or maybe she loathed Mimi, too!

I am not a monster, Mimi thought. I love my child, my cruel child. Don't be so impatient, Bill would chide her, don't jump to conclusions. Think about what's happened, what you might have done. But Bill was not here. Bill was dead. Mimi could bounce straight from shame to revenge, and no one to make her wallow in the middle, where the murky questions lay.

Jean tied Boo to a lamppost and went inside the hotel with Marc, his arm resting lightly on her shoulder. When she was sure they had gone upstairs, Mimi came out from the shadows. Swiftly she untied Boo and started back with him—to the corner, then right, and down the long blocks to Taraval. When Jean returned, pale and distraught, Mimi would ask no questions, provide no defense, make no accusations. She would tell her daughter that the dog had wandered home on his own. She had found him scratching at the door, lonely and scared, and she had let him in. Swiftly, clutching the leash, she retraced her steps down the alphabet, her eyes on fire.

Old Man

WHITEN YOUR TEETH. Color your hair. Get a facial—no, she meant a real facial, glycolic acid peel. Maybe an eyelid tuck.

Thus his sister, Mattie, talked to Scott. "People do these things," she said.

"Guys?"

"Guys do them, yes. If they want it bad enough."

Scott pressed his thumb and forefinger to his untucked eyelids. Unemployed for nineteen months, he had just come home from his weekly meeting of MBA, Managers Between Assignments. His wife, Peg, was in the kitchen, breathing disapproval. Mattie had come by to talk about the Judge, but she couldn't resist giving Scott advice.

"You could give up smoking," she said. "That would at least stop your teeth from getting any browner."

"Please," Scott said in a low tone. "My little vice. Already Peg won't let me, in the house."

"Oh well. If Peg says no."

Mattie could flip from one side to the other of an argument, depending on who was fronting the opposition. When their mother was alive, she'd pushed for the exercise program at the community center. When Scott complained that Mom was never ready at pickup time, Mattie decided the whole exercise routine was a crock.

Scott was fifty, four years short of the age when, he had once boasted to Mattie, he planned to retire. He'd made the boast back when he was approaching the two-decade mark at Midstate Bank. "Risen in the ranks," he used to say at church picnics. "Company man."

Then he had gotten a call from a head-hunter out of Chicago, looking for a "man on the ground" for a Midwestern branch set-up. He wasn't looking for a job, Scott had said at first. But he would run the show. Lease and furnish the office space, hire the staff. Huge corp, Allied Trust, and they were looking for a fellow exactly like Scott. When you're good, the head-hunter had said, the work finds you.

"Take a risk, for once in your life," Mattie had said.

Eight months, and they laid him off. They had rethought the concept. Maybe better to base out of Indianapolis, where they had a guy already in place. Scott could relocate to New York, but he'd need six months' training, and he couldn't expect, and they wouldn't promise, and Scott stopped listening after not very much of this yap.

In his den he had the rocking chair Midstate gave at retirement—a joke it had been, at the farewell party, that Scott had earned his rocker and he would rock, goddammit, even if he was bounding off to greener pastures. It sat across from the leather couch he'd bought the week he started at Allied Trust, the salary differential in a month enough to pay for the thing, and they'd thrown in the Barcalounger. Mattie was perched cross-legged on the couch. Scott rocked.

"This Monday group of yours," Mattie said now. "It wouldn't include any geriatric-care lawyers, would it?"

"Lawyers aren't out of work," said Scott.

"Because the Judge is going to need a lawyer," said Mattie.

"He will not need a lawyer." Scott could feel it inside, the slow, rising bubble of success. "Peg and I have a solution."

•

SCOTT WAS NAMED FOR THEIR FATHER, Francis Scott McGuire, Judge McGuire, who was never Francis or Scott but plain old Judge to his closest friends. Five times in the Judge's career, the gathered attorneys of St. Louis County had voted him unfit due to a lack of judicial temperament. Each time, the voters, who loved a handsome face, had reinstalled him. That particular dance had finished twenty-one years ago, since which time the

Judge had enjoyed the career for which he had trained: professional Old Man. You couldn't talk to him without a three-minute speech on deafness and the proper way to address a deaf person. He reserved the right to nap at any hour of the day, and to demand Campbell's Beef & Barley in place of any meal that was served. At eighty-six, pressured by his second wife, Lucille, and by his children, he had conferred with Jesus and determined that to put his loved ones' minds at ease, he would give up driving. This generous resolution had not prevented his sneaking out at night in the Fairlane and tooling down to the Half-Pint for a draught Bud. Only when Mattie, perpetually broke, put on her humble hat and begged the Judge for a set of wheels did he part with the car and the keys and pronounce himself content to be chauffeured. "Do the Old Man a favor," he would say when he called.

Now the Judge had broken his left hip, and Lucille wanted to leave him where he was, at Barnes Extended Care. Surgery had gone well; the Judge believed he would be going home in a hundred days, as promised by the doctor. But Lucille had power of attorney. She was scurrying around, Scott knew, to get the Judge declared incompetent.

"The problem," Mattie said, "is that he's lived about a decade longer than she planned on."

"The problem," chimed Scott's wife, Peg, from the kitchen, "is that she's got ice in her veins."

Scott thought it took one to know one, but he didn't speak to that. Peg was angry with him all day, every day. She had been angry with him when he worked long hours for lousy money at Midstate. Then, soon enough, she was angry with him for leaving Midstate for a job he had kept only eight months. That he had failed to recapture his title at Midstate, or anywhere else, she found unforgivable. Every day. For nineteen months.

"I have a plan," said Scott, leaning in toward his sister. He craved a cigarette. "Come out on the deck," he said.

"I'm leaving for work!" Peg shouted as they were closing the

146

sliding door. "The kids need rides to their soccer practices!"

Scott lifted a hand, to let her know he'd heard. Then the door slid tight. He had installed it himself, along with the deck. Peg had no idea, he thought sometimes, no concept at all. He cupped his hand around the lighter and leaned down. It was a breezy day, April. Soccer would be muddy.

"A plan," Mattie repeated.

He took a drag and felt better. He motioned to Mattie to sit at the table, the picnic table he'd put together from a kit and sanded smooth. His heart started to beat faster. "Peg and I have been talking," he said. "You know how stressed she's been at the hospital."

Peg was a nurse. "If she didn't work such odd hours—" Mattie began.

Scott waved her off. "She's felt she had to do it for the over-time," he said. "Because I'm out of work."

"Which she reminds you of every thirty seconds," Mattie said.

"The point," said Scott, "is she's getting high blood pressure, plus that pinched nerve in her neck. She needs to take time off. And I am beginning to think God left me unemployed this long for a reason."

Mattie rolled her eyes. Like Scott, she had left the Episcopal church the minute she was confirmed in the faith. Unlike him, she had not married a Catholic. She could not understand how it surrounded you—the parish, the schools, all Peg's and Scott's friends wearing little gold crosses and talking about God as if he ran the firm they all worked for. Scott didn't admit to his sister that he had started to pray.

"It has enabled me," he went on, "to realize that Peg and I are ideally suited to take Dad on. I have the time, Peg has the training. We've spoken to the boys about it. They understand that this is the right thing to do."

"But this house—" Mattie began.

"I've been looking at houses. Found a couple already. One real beauty in Warson Woods, with a totally handicapped-accessible room and bath on the first floor. Not much land, but the boys are old enough—"

"You're going to buy a new house?" Mattie looked around the porch, the yard with its playset, the wood chimes. "You love this house."

"Peg's never liked it."

"*Peg*. You can't afford a new house."

"We would have to be compensated, obviously. But Dad would be with people who love him, and in a home with a resident registered nurse. Peg could cut back on her hours."

"If you were compensated, you mean."

"I'm going to find work, Matt. It's just a question of patience. If Peg is home more, and happier, in a new house, and Dad—"

"It's one-stop shopping, isn't it?" Mattie said. She reached for his pack of Winstons. He knew she would. "Peg gets a new house. You bring home some cabbage from the Judge. She stops bitching so much. Dad gets out of the nursing home. You get to be Number One son at last."

"You're saying there's something wrong with a plan because it works for everyone?" Scott stubbed out his cigarette. His smile felt like a shield.

"I am saying," mumbled Mattie as she cupped her palm around the lighter, "nothing works for everyone."

•

SCOTT DROPPED HIS THREE SONS—Frank, fifteen and built like a rock; Geoff, thirteen and surly; Colin, eight and frail as a girl—at their muddy fields. At Colin's practice he lingered. The day was hazy, the Ozark foothills indistinct as the songs Colin whispered to himself. Parents huddled at these younger kids' practices, crossing their arms over their windbreakers and trading tips. There were two other dads, both out of work. One had joined MBA. "Got a lead down at the university," he was saying as Scott stepped over. "Public relations. I talked to the outplacement people, and they think there might be transferable skills."

"Alums get those university jobs," said the other dad. "Or Blacks."

"Worth trying," said the first dad.

Scott didn't say anything. He could not imagine a job at a university in public relations. That was his problem, Peg had told him. He lacked imagination. He couldn't see himself doing anything besides what the bank had told him to do. He had been fired from Allied Trust, she insisted when her mood got really dark, not because they changed their game plan but because he had no imagination.

At the two-year mark, Peg had told him a month ago, she would boot him out. He could see how the leisure life suited him when he lived in a rented room.

But that was before the Judge broke his hip, before the Judge's ditz of a wife decided to have him declared incompetent. Before Scott came up with his solution.

"Tell me something, Scott," said the first dad, as Scott slid back into the van. "You getting any?"

"Pardon?" said Scott.

"You know. At home. From what I can tell, it's the first thing to go."

"Geez. That's too bad."

"So you're still getting some? After nineteen months?"

"Getting a little," said Scott, which was a lie.

•

THREE DAYS AFTER HE SPILLED THE PLAN to Mattie, they held the Meeting. Mattie had arranged it. They gathered in the Judge's living room—Scott, Mattie, Lucille, and the Geriatric Advisory Report, a garbled document in a bright blue folder. "Experts in the field," said Lucille, smoothing the cover, "prepared this report about your father."

Lucille had let her hair go white when she turned sixty, and she wore only cream-colored clothing, so with her round-framed glasses she looked like a snowy owl. For this occasion she had served up Cokes and Nestea. There was a plate of butter cookies with spots of dried strawberry jam in the center. She picked up the report and read aloud. This process was always difficult, the report maintained, for family members. Accepting the inevitable was not easy. Francis Scott McGuire, the report said, was a brilliant man. But he was having issues with his self care.

Scott had downed two Nesteas, and his throat still felt parched.

"I wanted you two to know," Lucille went on, "that I have explored a number of options. I asked the geriatric care consultant for a summary of your father's diagnosis. I have here several pages of alternative care plans. As you'll see"—she pulled out photocopies and handed them to Scott and Mattie—"the costs of in-home care at the level your father requires are prohibitive."

Scott studied the figures printed on the vellum stock. Lists marked by small, shadowed arrows cited the advantages and disadvantages of each option. The consultant's observations referred to the Judge as "Francis," which Scott found offensively personal. No one except Lucille called his father Francis, and it seemed presumptuous for a paid consultant to do so, especially in writing. But Scott didn't say this. He waited until Lucille had read the report aloud, all six pages of it. Clearing his throat, he said, "I disagree with this statement here, on page four."

They all rustled their sheets.

"Where it reads," Scott went on, "'Lucille and the children may *initially* experience feelings of guilt, loss, anger and failure if Francis stays at the nursing home.' Then we have what's labeled a personal note—I don't know this person—that these feelings are very normal and can be resolved. 'Very' is all caps."

"I asked them to add that information," said Lucille. She seemed to brighten at the personal note, which was printed in a different, slightly flowery font. Mattie, perched in one of Lucille's least comfortable chairs, a Queen Anne contraption upholstered in pink, pinched her lips together.

"I am glad to know these feelings are normal," said Scott. He was sitting on the edge of Lucille's couch, which the Judge had always complained about. Once you got in it, the Judge said, you needed a hoist to get out. Scott was not a tall man, and he was trying not to sink below the level of these women perched in their pastel chairs. "But I can guarantee you, Lucille," he said, "my feelings are not merely initial, and they are not apt to be resolved."

Behind her glasses, Lucille no longer looked like an owl. She looked like a fish asleep, lidless and blank. "They go by their experience with hundreds of families," she said after a long pause. "I asked if they advised counseling for family members. They said it might be indicated."

"Good for them," said Scott. He sat up further on the hard edge of the couch. His heart beat faster. There was a twang to Lucille's voice that reminded him of Peg, of Peg's tone of voice when she defended sending the boys to Catholic schools and would not be contradicted. But Lucille was Episcopalian, same as the Judge. He took a deep breath, and began. "My wife and I have an alternative to propose," he said. He glanced quickly at Mattie, then focused on Lucille.

"Yes?" she said.

"I have begun to believe God has left me unemployed for a reason," he said. Out of the corner he saw Mattie's eye-roll. "I want to help my father," he said. "My wife is a registered nurse. We have three children who love their grandfather. We have looked at several homes with handicapped accessibility."

Lucille seemed to have frozen. "Scott means like ramps, bathrooms, extra-wide doorways," Mattie put in helpfully.

"Yes," said Lucille.

"Now you can't—or you won't—bring your husband back home," said Scott. "But if he chooses not to stay where he is, he need not go begging for a home."

Lucille nodded. Her plump white hands lay folded in her lap. Scott pushed on. He explained how Peg would adjust her schedule, how she would train Scott and Frank to provide appropriate care for the Judge. How the Judge would thrive in a warm and loving family atmosphere. He described the house in Warson Woods. Out of the corner of his eye he could see his sister's mouth working, as if she were chewing gum. His voice grew tight in his throat.

"So you see," he said, "we have a plan, and we are prepared to execute it. Not because we have to. But because it is the *right* thing to do. This is what you do for family!"

With his right index finger he found he was jabbing at the soft arm cushion of the couch. His chin trembled a little. He sounded, he knew, like a pompous prick. But he'd caught Lucille unawares. He could tell that much. She nodded. She swallowed. She said "Well."

"It's incredibly generous of you, Scott," put in Mattie. "But—"

"It is not generous," he said. He felt for his cigarette pack in his shirt pocket, then let it go. "It is the *right thing*."

"Yes, and Lucille probably admires—"

"Nothing to admire," Scott said. Don't let them mollycoddle you, Peg had said as he left the house. Well, he wasn't going to be mollycoddled. "We are doing this for my *father*."

Lucille remained waxen-faced, listening as to a sermon. Jesus, he loathed the woman. For the Judge to go from their mother to this—!

"For my part," said Mattie, "I think it's great. But—"

"But nothing," said Scott.

"Let Matilda finish," said Lucille.

He bit the inside of his cheek.

"But Daddy can be one royal pain in the butt, Scott, and you've got a wife kicking you there already."

Jesus Christ, they were in cahoots. His father's little owl and his flip-flop of a sister. "We have discussed this," said Scott. "Peg and I are prepared for the challenge."

"Well," said Lucille. Her face brightened, though not enough

OLD MAN

to melt the wax. "As the guardian of your father, I will put this generous offer into the mix. More tea, Scott?"

Waving her off, Scott took a cookie. He sat back on the couch. He didn't care, for a minute or two, how deep he sank.

•

THE FOLLOWING MONDAY he loitered in the back at the MBA meeting. When Scott had first heard about MBA, they'd numbered a couple dozen white guys over forty. Now you could barely fit into the room for the weekly Danish, and they had started charging for the coffee. This week's speaker was talking about transition to information technologies, but Scott couldn't tune in. He studied the coiffed heads in the plastic chairs, under the rust-stained acoustic tiles, desperate people acting polite. What good were any of them to the world? They were all, more or less, like Scott—children who had reached adulthood with all the right credentials but no passions worth mentioning. Mattie was right—three of them, he counted, had colored their hair. Trying to wind the clock backward. Well he, Scott McGuire, had passions.

Yesterday he had taken Peg through the house in Warson Woods. The realtor had stood back and let them wander the rooms, and he had seen how happy his wife could become. "It's in the same parish," she had marveled as they drove home. That afternoon, the boys over at friends' houses, they had made love while rain spattered the windows. Peg had a tight, muscular body, her belly looser from the births and her thighs spidered with veins, but her back as strong, her breasts as rounded as when they first met.

He wanted to be of use. He wanted—tears came to Scott's eyes as he thought this, and he took a quick sip of his coffee, to steady his nerves—to come to his loved ones bearing the gifts for which they had been praying.

"You all right, fella?" said another guy lingering in the back.

"Allergies," said Scott, pushing up on his lower eyelid.

"Gets you coming and going, don't it?" the guy said.

153

Scott set down his coffee and looked at his watch. "I got an interview," he said.

"Hey! You lucky bastard!" The guy raised his coffee in a toast. "Break a leg," he said.

Quick trip down Highway 40, same route he used to take to Midstate Bank. Same exit, even. The cars poured onto Brentwood Boulevard. And then the industrial park with its goose-infested pond, and the green-roofed building with his father inside.

His mother had been here too—a short while. She was not one to linger, like the Judge. "My son," she would introduce him to the staff. "Vice president at Midstate." The staff person would raise her eyebrows and say, "*Very* nice." Though they all knew, surely, that Midstate had a couple dozen vice presidents in St. Louis alone. "Don't hide your lamp under a bushel," his mother would say when he protested. What lamp, you had to wonder. What lamp was she talking about?

He finished his cigarette and stubbed it out in the gray sand of the tray outside the sliding doors. Striding through the lobby, he winked and waved at the obese receptionist, then punched the elevator for the third floor. It was when the Judge was moved to the third floor that Scott's solution had begun to crystallize. The third floor was where people died, in this place. And he had seen the psychiatrists Lucille had brought in, both of them Jewish guys with peppery hair and rimless glasses, ready to pronounce incapacitation, dementia, delirium, incompetence.

"Dad," he said. He strode into the room. The Judge lay on his back on the hospital bed, his good leg crooked, his frail one straight as a peg under the sheet. He was asleep. He breathed, as usual, through his mouth, open wide as a nutcracker's; Scott could see the back sides of his long incisors. His skin stretched over his bones. On his right hand, resting on his thigh, the veins braided themselves like tree roots. The white hair sprouted from his head. It would not be much of a stretch to picture him as a shrunken head, hung on the rafter of a hut in Africa

154

to ward off ghosts. But he breathed; he was alive. "How're you doing, Dad?" Scott asked.

The Judge slept. Scott ate the yogurt left untouched from the hospital breakfast. He flicked on Fox News. He spoke to Mattie on his cell phone; she was in rehearsal. "Lucille called me last night," she said. "She's not going to let you get away with this."

"She is not going to stop me," said Scott.

"Scott, I have to say, it is a dumb idea. I mean, I didn't tell Lucille this, but your situation is not going to be helped by having a senile Southern aristocrat dominating your household."

"I need to do what's best, Mattie."

"Knock the halo off. You need to get your teeth whitened and get your Series 6, is what you need. And maybe some dermabrasion."

He hung up as the nurse came in.

"Time for your medicine, Judge," she said, and the old man woke.

"Ah ee uh ah-uh," he said.

"He needs some water," the nurse translated, though Scott already knew. He poured from the plastic pitcher into the plastic cup, and held it for his father.

"Thank you," said the Judge. "Now, what's this woman want?"

"Time for your meds," the nurse repeated. She was a pockmarked Jamaican with square shoulders. Severely straightened, her hair was pinned against her head like a ball of waxed string. She spoke with a lilt that seemed to annoy the Judge.

"I think she wants me to take something," the Judge said to Scott. "Can't you come back later?" he said loudly to the nurse.

"I already gone away and come back twice," she lilted. "You got to take the pills now."

"I am a deaf person, in case you have not noticed," said the Judge. "If I put my hearing aids in, I will understand you better. Face me when you speak. You must speak very loudly, and very slowly. This is true for many old people. Do you understand me?"

"Yes, Mr. McGuire," said the nurse.

"All right. Proceed with what you were saying."

"You have got to take your pills. Now," said the nurse. Her voice was firm, like Peg's, but less bright. Patients liked his wife, Scott often reminded himself; they found her sharpness cheerful.

"No sense of timing, these people," the Judge was saying to Scott. "I think I need to have a BM."

"We will do that," the nurse said. "After these pills."

The Judge leaned toward Scott and shielded his mouth with his bony hand. "She is the stupidest colored woman," he said in a stage whisper.

"Just take your medications, Dad," Scott said. He smiled at the nurse, to let her know he was not in cahoots with his father. This would be easier with Peg, in the new house.

"Big ones first," the nurse said. In her hand she held a narrow tray lined with a dozen pills, varied in color and size. With a tiny spoon she fished out an oval peach-colored tablet.

"That's the kind gets stuck in my throat," said the Judge. "I've got to open wide for it. Lucille had to execute a Heimlich maneuver on me once, did you know that?"

"I heard about that," said Scott.

"You ready?" said the nurse. She winked at Scott.

"On three," said the Judge.

She rocked the spoon back and forth. "One," she said. "Two, three." But the Judge's lips were pinched tight.

"Wasn't ready!" he said. Charged with static, his white hair stood up like ruffled feathers. His eyes were small, paler than Scott remembered them, with lids thin as rice paper.

"We try again," said the nurse.

"I need to have a BM," said Scott's father. He pushed himself up on the bed. The top of his pajamas was unbuttoned, and Scott could see his caved-in chest, the hollow below his breastbone, his tiny belly.

"I think you'd better let him," Scott said.

The nurse sighed. She set the tray of pills on top of the wheat-colored dresser. "Can you transfer, Mr. McGuire?" she asked.

"What's she want now?" the Judge asked Scott.

"Wants to be sure you'll use your walker!" shouted Scott.

"Walk her?" said the Judge. "That woman?"

"This!" Scott laid hold of the gray walker by the end of the bed and shook it.

It would be easier, in the new house. If Lucille would let them take the Judge away from here, and the Judge would give them the funds. If the Judge didn't die first.

"I have told you people," said the Judge, his thin legs now dangling over the side of the bed. "I learned my lesson with that fall. I shall not make the same mistake again. Now you people need to get off my back! I tell Lucille all the time! She treats me like some kind of Mongolian idiot! Now give me that thing."

Scott set the walker up, and the Judge rose.

•

AT HOME, PEG HAD JUST WOKEN; Colin was home from school. Together they sat at the kitchen table, Peg with her coffee and a warm compress against her neck, Colin with the grilled cheese sandwich that only Mommy made right. "Hey, Dad," said Colin as Scott came in. He tolerated a kiss on his forehead, as did Peg. This was their time together—not a time Frank or Geoff had needed with their mother, but Colin was the youngest and most—well, girlish was the word that came to mind. He liked to chatter with Peg, to sing her the songs to which he knew all the words.

Scott stepped down to his office, the space he'd carved out of the basement, walled off and carpeted. He booted up the computer, logged on to Monster.com, and set to filtering out possibilities. There was something in Springfield; he could commute to Springfield. Evanston. Kansas City—now that was a stretch. But if they moved to Warson Woods, with the Judge, and the salary was enough to keep Peg home full-time…. His family might rather he be gone during the week. The house could hum along, three boys and their mother and a crotchety patient.

Upstairs, the muffled voices ceased. After a minute, Peg's light tread on the steps. "Anything?" she asked.

"Loan officer. Customer service."

"Colin wants voice lessons. They're thirty an hour."

Scott snorted. "I'll teach him to sing."

"You can't hold a tune." She came to look over his shoulder. "My neck hurts."

He reached up to massage it, but she moved out of range.

"There's something," she said, pointing to the screen.

"Annuities," said Scott. "I'd need a Series 6 license."

Peg leaned against the table on which Scott had neatly stacked job descriptions, resumes, brochures. Her blue robe was tied loosely, her face still shiny with night cream. She slept in four- and ten-hour stretches, depending on the day; she never looked completely rested. "You remember how Frank used to lose his baseball cap?" she said.

"Which one?" Scott scrolled down the screen. He'd seen all these already.

"Signed by no-relation McGuire. You know. When he'd lose it, he wouldn't wear another one. It drove us all nuts. Then he left it behind on a class field trip, remember? To Meremac Caverns? I got in a yelling match with him. I told him that cap was gone, gone, gone. He shut himself in his room for a whole day. Then he came out and put on a different cap." She gestured at the screen. "You won't find your Midstate job again," she said. "You'll have to learn to wear a new cap."

"Or you'll leave."

Peg untied her robe, then tightened it. "How's the Judge?"

"Dying, unless we get him out of there."

"I thought Lucille wouldn't hear of it."

"She'll hear of it. We'll get an attorney."

"That Warson Woods house won't wait for an attorney."

"Peg. Honey." He left the screen and swiveled his chair. Before she could pull away, he took both her small hands in his. "It will work," he said, "but I'm not the only one who needs to let an old cap go."

But Peg was stubborn. "Yes, you are," she said. Her voice barely shook.

•

AT LEAST, SCOTT THOUGHT as he left to pick Frank up at school, he had sired boys. Whatever happened in his life, he would not be surrounded forever by women. He had wanted some closeness with his father, truth be told, mainly as defense against the females who swarmed around them—Mattie, Peg, Lucille, the nurses. Eventually his father would come to see that Scott was his best resort. In the house in Warson Woods, his father would rest in the Barcalounger while Scott put up bookshelves, and together they would figure how to get Frank into a decent college. In the end, the Judge would say to Scott, "I underestimated you, son. You were the one I should have counted on, all the way through." And then the Judge would pass on to his reward, and Scott would assume his mantle.

He would have a job by then, surely. Once his father moved in, Scott couldn't help thinking, an offer would follow. He could wear any cap that fit, darn it. The world simply had not reached the point where intelligent, upstanding white fathers resorted to Botox in order to support their families.

Parking the van in the line-up of cars, Scott bent his head. "Dear Lord," he said aloud, "grant that my father may come to share a new home with us, and that my wife will be satisfied with me. If it be your wishes, Amen."

He stepped out of the car and stretched his back. The sun was out from a scrim of clouds, already soaking the black asphalt hot. The cars gleamed in their colors, like a gigantic row of pills. Inside them, or leaning on the doors, waited the mothers, gossiping with one another or on their cell phones. Standing silent, its white cross held aloft, the school waited to disgorge its swarm of restless children, yearning to be adults and free.

From the other side of the lot, a man approached. He extended his hand. Scott recognized him vaguely, from the MBA meetings, and nodded familiarly when the man introduced himself, John something.

"Hear you're looking at houses," John said.

"Checking around," said Scott. "We might—my father's coming to live with us."

"Tough luck," said John. Scott tried to figure if he colored his hair. Very brown on the top, but gray sideburns. He decided not.

"No," said Scott. "We welcome him."

"Well, I bit the bullet," said John. He squinted in the sun. "Got my real estate license. Now I'm my own man."

"No kidding. You like it?"

"Love it," said John, though Scott didn't believe the smile the fellow flashed at him. "Anyhow, thought I might help you out. Got a couple places to show. Give you my card."

"Great," said Scott. He took the card—blue embossed with gold lettering, pretentious—and tucked it into his wallet.

"You still looking?"

"Still looking?" Scott reached into his shirt pocket, touched his pack of cigarettes, left it there. So much time everything took! Time to find a job, time to buy a house, time to circumvent Lucille, time for his father to die. From behind the line of cars, he heard the shouts of liberated teenagers. When was it—not that long ago—it seemed a snap of his fingers could make things change? *Patience is a virtue*, the Judge used to say every time the lawyers voted to boot him out. *Possess it if you can.*

"I'm not looking," Scott said to this beaming, brown-haired John, "so much as praying. You know." He made a joke of it. "Praying to be found."

The Road Taken

BEFORE SHE WENT OVER THE CLIFF, she had been thinking about Frost. The lesson plan called for her to teach his poem "The Road Not Taken" in the usual, Emersonian way: as the brave choice of the individual to choose the path untrod and so make a difference in the world. Such bullshit. She'd studied Frost, damn it, and she knew how tricky and ornery the guy was. First of all, it wasn't like there were paths laid out and you just chose them. He said so, in the poem: the path you take is the path you make, you become that path, and so the whole two-path scheme is nonsense. Second, the paths looked the same. There wasn't one less trod than the other. You were just going to make that story up for your grandchildren, to make yourself look interesting.

It was shitting rain. Had been raining for three days straight. This journey, not a path but Highway 1 north from Santa Rosa to Mendocino, was not the road she wanted to take at all. But here she was, rounding another of the curves that bellied out over the Pacific then dove deep into a ravine. On a sunny day, her eyes couldn't adjust fast enough from the glare over the blue water to the gloom of the ravines, so for a few seconds she drove blind into the darkness until she made out the waterfall cutting its way, then the road jackknifed back and up into the glare. Today wasn't one of those days. The wipers whipped at their highest speed. She was thinking what an asshole Dennis was. She was thinking she'd turn around at the boat landing a half-mile north. She'd go back to the apartment and give him what for. Then she executed the turn and the car entered a mud slide. *Turn into the skid*, she told herself, Minnesota drivers' training, and into the skid she went, and no guardrails, the cliff, and what were you supposed to do when the skid went off the road, but too late for questions, and she went over. Three hundred feet down, the front bumper smacked a boulder, her head smacked the windshield. No one saw her go. The rain poured down for three more days before they found her.

This story isn't about me. I'm gone.

Give me a child until he is seven, and I will show you the man.

•

THERE'S ONLY ONE ROAD not taken. The road I would have taken, choice upon choice. None of which matter a fig to me now, of course. What I am vouchsafed to know is the source of that nagging feeling—you've experienced it, everyone has—that someone was supposed to arrive. The flip side of *déja vu*; let's call it *devrais voir*.[1] That you're not in the right house, not eating the dinner you're meant to be eating. This argument with your wife—it's not the real argument, she's not your real wife, this house you lovingly restored brick by brick and circuit breaker by circuit breaker ought to be someone else's. You weren't meant to get a bichon frise. Yeah, Rupert's adorable, but seriously? Isn't there a horse in the picture? Or an aquarium filling the wall between the two picture windows in downtown Austin, not that you like fish, but she and the kids take care of them and it's pretty to watch, late at night, when depression hits and you turn on the torchière in the living room and settle on the couch to listen to Arvo Pärt. Wait. Aren't you supposed to be in Roanoke, Virginia? Jesus, whoever thought of *Roanoke*?

You, for instance. Neal. It's another rainy day, only in New York City. You've just broken off with Elizabeth. Remember Elizabeth? So perfectly blond, day job on Wall Street but no particular ambitions, big Episcopalian family in Concord, Massachusetts. Twenty-five, and she still hasn't gotten over Simon, the British architect she met on her junior year abroad. She lets you have sex with her; if you hang in there, maybe

[1] French for "should be seeing." There's a soupçon of French in this story; don't be offended.

162

she'll even marry you, and you'll have blond twins and buy a house in Westchester, but you can't stand it that she doesn't love you.[2] Warm rain, early June, light until late. You've just started a new job in sales, thanks to your brother Billy who knows you've got some confidence issues but you project well, winning smile, quick wit, maybe it'll work. But you don't want to go back to your apartment, not yet. There's life out here, in the rain, where the taxis gleam like yellow beachballs and spray the sidewalks to make dogs shimmy and couples jump together like dancing partners.

You duck, then, into a bookstore. The bookstore where we would have met. I would have left Dennis, of course. When they'd have fished me out of the gorge and taken me to the hospital in Santa Rosa, he wouldn't even get his ass up to visit for twenty-four hours because he was busy meditating. If you ask me, they were a bunch of selfish, self-righteous bastards, those transcendental types of 1980. I'd married him in a weak moment. I haven't followed him much since my death. I know he took his oh-so-capitalist trust fund and went to live in Japan. Either way, he thinks of me nostalgically, like a summer romance fated to pass away when the cold came.

I haven't followed you, either, until this moment. It's completely serendipitous. Often, at weddings, people bring up the first meeting, the chance encounter. (Well, not so much anymore, with Tinder and Match, but once upon a time, lives collided.) What if she hadn't gone shopping for flowers that day? What if he hadn't walked into that bar? For me, time has accordioned. There is no "what if" because the whole thing either happened or didn't happen, all at the same time. More a painting, you might say, than a symphony. But here we are, in the bookstore, and it's not happening. I'm not coming in, dripping wet, shaking my umbrella by the entrance. I'm not asking the bored-looking woman behind the counter where

2 What is love? Don't those Pakistani couples who meet on their wedding night have as good a chance at happiness as any of Cupid's victims? You refuse to think about this.

the Hollywood books are. I'm not weaving my way to the poorly lit back of the store and crouching down by Tinseltown biographies. You're not following me, racking your brain for a topic of conversation, pushing Elizabeth out of your head for once and all.

No. What you do, instead—after glancing up every time the door chimes, as if you're expecting your future to bustle in from the wet street—is to buy a birthday card for your nephew. You don't know why you're doing this. He's only eight months old, for Chrissake. You don't know that's the lie you were going to give me, to account for your lingering so long by the card rack at the bookstore, trying to snag a thread of conversation. Anyway, it's a cute card, a steam engine on the front with wheels the kid can spin, and you'll put it on the shelf in your apartment and forget about it.

The rain stops. Sun steams the sidewalk. Restless, dissatisfied, you continue up Second Avenue. Somehow, in that little bookstore, the decision's been made: you'll stop chasing after Elizabeth. Climbing the stairs to your apartment, you've practically forgotten about her. After you've cracked a beer, you call your brother Frank—not the father of the nephew, but your twin, so like and unlike you in every way, both of you tall and clever but Frank steady as a rock and Neal mercurial as lightning. "You watching the game tonight?" you ask.

Which was the same thing you asked the evening after we met, so let's not pause here. Let's riffle forward a few pages, to where you've met and moved in with Diana. I hate to think how promising this is. Diana's ten years older than you, divorced with a kid, sexy in a blousy way. She runs a fitness center, Total Life, in Brooklyn; she's a lot more efficient than she looks. But hungry, oh so hungry, baby, and she laughs at your jokes with a laugh that starts deep down by her Cesarean incision and makes its way up past her generous breasts with their large, dark brown aureoles to where she shakes her corkscrew curls, colored auburn to hide the gray creeping in.

"She's got you pussy-whipped," says Frank after you've moved in with Diana and lost your job[3] and started working at Total Life part time and doing kid duty the rest of it.

"I'm into the kink," you say. Though you know Frank's not talking about sexual habits. All the brothers share this fear. Not that your crazy alcoholic mom controlled your stalwart alcoholic dad. But that none of you knows how to be married and the women know, and that gives them a terrifying amount of power. The great thing about Diana is that her age is a little bruise in the muscle. She's looking forty in the eye. When you get to forty, she'll be looking at fifty. Let gratitude be her watchword.

Will you get her pregnant? No. Though she wants another one bad, right now, at forty and with you. But as you and I both know, your sperm count is ridiculously low. You tell her this the same way you'd have told me: after the knot's been tied and the hopes have risen. Now and then, despite the good sense visiting you, you feel the hankering to commit to a varicocele operation, which (as I know and you don't) would swell your gonads to a painful and alarming proportion. But lucky you, she already has Claire—that's the kid, a girl, we always said you should have had girls, and Claire proves it, you're completely enchanted by her, you play endless games of Uno with her, and when she makes it all the way across the monkey bars the thrill surpasses that time you won States in the hundred meter, when you were seventeen.[4] Claire's real dad moved back to Argentina four years ago. So he exists, but not as a threat. When people

3 I'm sorry to report that your habit of getting fired persists, despite my absence from your life. Remember that quote about the seven-year-old boy? That's Ignatius Loyola, founder of the Jesuits, the order of the Catholic school your alcoholic parents sent you to. The good saint says once we're formed in early childhood, we are who we are for the rest of our lives. In which case it doesn't matter which path we take–or, rather, we don't choose paths arbitrarily. Frost was never going to take that other winding way in the woods. You were never going to settle for Elizabeth. I couldn't have avoided Dennis.

4 The year your mom failed to get you treatment for the hernia that almost axed your fertility. Seventeen isn't seven, but the principle holds. Every tendency taps to a deep root.

stop you on the street to marvel at your adorable little girl, you take every ounce of the credit.

My job, you might say, is to get out of the way now. Plenty of others have failed, like me, to cross your path. I'm not talking about Mr. Spangler, who would have been your sixth-grade teacher and might have given you more confidence than Father John stole from you, had Spangler's wife not contracted terminal cancer and insisted on moving close to her family. I'm talking only about people on the knife-edge of death and life who slip toward death. They're telling their stories right now. They detect those nanoseconds when you miss them, when you know that if they had only been there....but what of them and their alternate worlds? I have access only to this one life of yours, the one whose missing ingredient is yours truly. Yours truly who, after she left Dennis and moved East, would have met you in that bookstore. But hell's bells, she didn't make it.

Nor can the products of what never happens be part of our consideration. By which I mean, mostly, our two sons. However fiercely we'd have loved them, whatever joys and sorrows they'd have brought—and let's be honest, having kids, especially Tristan, broke us apart—they can't exist without me, so they're not worth talking about. Timing, place, other people make the soup that expresses predilection as action. With me, you'd have taken measures, brought two heartbreaking kids into the world. With Diana, there's Claire. Don't ask about Elizabeth, you opted out of Elizabeth. Same you, different life; different life, different man; same man you were always going to be, no matter the whiff of *what if.*

You screw around, of course. You always have, with women. Every few months, you have to put your attractiveness to the test. That you would have remained faithful to me constitutes a startling anomaly[5] and can't apply to the situation with Diana except insofar as you've paused, once or twice, to feel the loss

---

5 Until the end, at least. Those last few months, when I'd already have left with the boys and you would try so hard to pull it together and bring us back. Nothing I'd ever begrudge you. And on my part? This is not about my part.

of someone to be faithful *to*. And what an odd word, *faithful*. Better to say *exclusive*. You never feel you've broken faith with her.

Let's consider, for instance, Valerie.

You tell it.

•

OKAY, LET'S GET THIS OFF MY CHEST. Diana and I have been together eight years, married for six.[6] We're friends more than lovers. We live in Carroll Gardens, in a duplex she got as part of her divorce settlement. Everything good about our life comes from her. But I get restless. Pent up. So one day last spring I'm bicycling to work, and I pass the new bakery going up on Court Street. Every day I've been passing it, seeing this girl—okay, woman—just the curvy side of slender, her hair chopped short as a boy's, in overalls, directing the renovations. I'd been shouting things out—*Got any donuts yet? Dig that baby blue! When do you finish? I'm hungry!* This time, she was squatting on the curb in the May sun, her head in her hands. I pulled up, slipped my ring onto the other hand, and squatted next to her.

"It can't be that bad," I said.

"They found *asbestos*," she said.

Which I knew was that bad. I put my arm across her shoulders, like we'd been intimate for months already. "You can get city money for that," I said. Which I *thought* was true, but of course I'd never tried. I manage one of Diana's five Total Life locations. I'm handy. When there's a leak in one of the locker rooms, I can get under the sink or behind the shower head and suss it out. But I've never actually built anything. Sometimes I think I'd like to, but a voice in my head tells me I'd fuck it up.[7]

"I'm Neal," I said, holding out my ringless hand.

"Valerie," she said.

---

6 Nine and seven, actually. You lie about your age now, too, though never about Diana's. Women love it that you're married to someone older. Automatic feminist.

7 Am I that voice? I can't take credit. I only observe. It's true that the kitchen fire taking down our beautiful home would have started in the lousy wiring you'd have installed when you gutted and rebuilt it. I would've tried to forgive you for it. I would've failed.

I lift her up and she dusts herself off, a round ass under the overalls, and she agrees to show me around the place which is mostly sawdust and exposed beams at that point. Over the next couple of weeks, I take to stopping by. Sometimes I bring *her* a muffin, just as a joke. Her green eyes set wide beside a shallow bridge of a nose, cheeks plump for a thin girl. When I get her back to her place and clothes off, maybe the middle of June, I'm astonished by the tattoos. A huge butterfly in the middle of her back. Twin trees up the back of her thighs, their branches and leaves spreading over her butt cheeks. I'm hooked.

Not to mention the pastries. She went to pastry school in Paris. I try my lame French on her, and when she laughs her eyebrows wiggle. I took a semester out from college, I tell her, to live in Paris, with my brother Gerald who was playing basketball over there. For the first time ever, I tell her how lonely I was in that city, how Gerald's place in La Défense felt like an asteroid hovering outside the real city, how I walked the rainy streets like a ghost until the metro stopped running and then I walked out of the glitter and across the bridge, traffic streaming by and then the colorless buildings in Neuilly hiding all that money, then nothing but wet skyscrapers and this thing that looked like the top half of a giant's picture frame rammed into the ground, it made me want to hike up onto the railing of the bridge and just let myself tip over into the black water. If I'd just known someone who spoke French, I said, who lived on the Left Bank or something, maybe I would have fallen in love with the city the way other people do. I was eating a cream puff and I started to cry, and she stroked my hair and then I went down on her.[8]

Finally they cleared up the asbestos—I don't know where Valerie got the money[9]—and the shop opened. *Allez-y Pastry*, which Valerie said was a pun so Americans would pronounce it *a lazy pastry*. Of course Claire wanted to go. I wouldn't take

8 You would never admit this loneliness to me. So yeah, there are things I'd never know, even if I'd made it out of that gorge. A lot of things.

9 From the city! You nailed it! Trumpet fanfare!

her. I made up every excuse. And she turned on me. She was eight then. Maybe she had a little baby fat. I don't know. One night she says to Diana, "Neal says I can't get macaroons at Lazy because I'm a tub of lard. I *hate* him." I don't know if I said that to her. It's an awful thing to say to a kid.[10] One thing led to another, and Diana was going to kick me out anyway, so I thought what the fuck and I told her. And you know what? Best thing I ever did. Turns out some people would rather you screw around on them than be mean to their child. Duh.

Valerie was another story. All I'll say is that the day I walked into the place—and it was beautiful, really a perfect shop, smelling like heaven, with art on the walls and a rack of books in the corner, and everything in the display cases lighter than clouds—with Claire at my side and my left hand up, palm facing in as if I was reading my own future so anyone who wanted could see the ring—the day I walked in like that, the world caved a little.

Six months later, the place was up for lease. A neighbor heard the owner moved to France. I hope she's happy there. If you want me to say I was a shit bag, okay, I was a shit bag. But Diana and I were okay. It hadn't been the first time, and it wasn't going to be the last. I'm not sure what I was looking for. We went to a marriage counselor a few times—not over Valerie, some other stuff—who said I courted risk.[11] This counselor claimed it was a sign of insecurity. I said to Diana after, "We paid her two hundred bucks to tell me that? We could've just asked my brothers."

•

Wow. So YOU DON'T ACTUALLY KNOW, about Valerie. How she went into the bathroom at the back of the kitchen after she saw you like that, with your daughter, and vomited her stomach empty. How she followed you, heartsick, along the streets of

10 You said it.

11 Manifested by your furious run at the stock market in the late 90s, with the insurance money we'd have gotten after you burned the house down. Who loses money in a rising market? Okay. I won't answer that.

Brooklyn. Neglected her business. Got guys to pound it out of her, all the love and hope, until sure enough she found a guy who gave her herpes, and that was just the beginning of the spiral.

What I mean is: even without me, you're not the nicest guy. (See: Loyola.) But you are safer, and you'll go farther. Diana will learn to tolerate the dalliances; she knows what happens when men reach their 60s and the testosterone slacks off. The marriage counselor recommends another therapist, who reminds you what an elastic life you have. You know how you used to carry a little pouch of charcoals and a pad around with you everywhere? Now you leave the gym a couple hours early. (It runs itself, really.) You take the sketchbook down to the park. You capture women and children, Italian grandmothers with their thick socks, bongo drummers, the old men at chess. People come up to talk. They nod appreciatively at what you've rendered; they detect your fundamental sympathy with the world. Every stroke of the charcoal, then the pen, then the brush, conveys desire.

You venture further. To the airport, where travelers sink disconsolately onto their suitcases and small children pull impatiently at sleeves. At dawn to the wharves where thick-palmed men haul in the day's catch. To the warehouses of Gowanus—that green canal!—and Red Hook, to the Hasidim in Crown Heights. Diana encourages you. You take a few classes. You're painting, now. Leaving the real outlines of the streets and vendors behind, fusing color to feeling. Next thing you know you're showing, in Manhattan. One dealer in Paris even takes you, and you go back there, avoiding La Défense and staying on the Left Bank, in view of a roofless Notre Dame—almost destroyed, you shudder somehow to think, by fire.[12] Your brothers can't believe the change. You've never made a wise choice in your life, but here you are.

12 I spoke fluent French, as you don't quite recall. Before we'd have met, while you were visiting Gerald, I spent a year on the Left Bank. Now, walking down Boulevard St.-Germain, your ears perk as you pass a café where a middle-aged woman with an American accent is *bavardé*ing. But you can't pick her out. As if she's a shadow.

Who knows what tapped the artist in you, the one that would have lain buried if my car had rammed into mud and not a boulder? We can't say it was Diana, or Valerie. Maybe living in Brooklyn, with all those pop-up galleries. Maybe the flex hours. Maybe the car that ran a light and knocked you sideways, shattering your left hip—you still hobble, a little—and reminding you that this ain't a dress rehearsal. But once you broke the surface, you burgeoned into glory, circumstances be damned.

Listeners always ask, what about me? There is no me. This nonsense about the lives they would have lived, if only, if only. Those lives don't exist. No road not taken.

Still I want to believe you miss something that we would call *me*, if we could. A part that's a little bit crazy. Remember that time you took Diana to your family place on Cape Cod, while your mother was still alive? You were far, far out on the flats, with a half-hour to go before the tide began seeping back in. You turned. You spotted her just off the beach, among the horseshow crabs. She's wearing a floppy yellow hat. You want to do something madcap. You're waiting for the signal. Then she turns to your sister in law and starts chatting, their voices too far to carry out to you. The rest of the day, you're crabby. In a funk. You pick a fight with your mom, who's three sheets to the wind already, and she spits at you—really embarrassing, and you go down to the beach under the stars and pitch rocks into the dark water.

What you miss—you can almost see it, smell it, taste it—is my loping out toward you, slowly flapping my arms like seagull wings. You miss how, when we got close, I pulled off my hat (not floppy yellow; a baseball cap we'd bought on the Blue Ridge, hiking) and flung it onto the sand. How you then ripped off your T-shirt and flung it. I did the same. You pulled off your swim trunks. I unhooked my bikini top, let the wind take it. All the while we kept moving toward each other, eyes on each other, until we flew together and you looped your arms around

171

my ass, my legs around your torso, and we stumbled with the impact until we collapsed on the wet sand. Laughing, laughing. We were far out from the beach. Onlookers would've had to reach for binoculars to make out our nakedness. Still, your family was pissed. They blamed me, of course. But you and I will always know that it wasn't me, it was we, it was our private craziness, and oh the pleasure of that contact, warm skin, salt.

You do miss that, don't you? That neighborhood in you that I would have inhabited—that, in a way, I still inhabit. That wild garden. I unlock the gates to it, but it can't be said that I turn the plants to savagery, to the carnivorous. That would be you. Living outside the garden, you miss only its splendor, not your wreckage. And in the midst of our *jouissance* (French again!), you'd have felt another touch, like a feather on the back of your neck. Claire, maybe. Or the gouache hanging in your study, sand strewn with blurry, colorful bits that look like clothing. The hazelnut coffee that Diana, silver-haired, slope-breasted, brings you now in bed. All our other paths are laid in leaves no step has trodden black. They thread our dreams.

ABOUT THE AUTHOR

Lucy Ferriss grew up in St. Louis, where her memoir, *Unveiling the Prophet*, is set. She attended Pomona College (BA) and San Francisco State University (MA) in California. She worked for Black Sparrow Press and in New York City publishing for several years. She taught at Harvard and Tufts universities, Hollins College, and Hamilton College before accepting an ongoing Writer-in-Residence position at Trinity College in Hartford. She has received a number of awards for her writing—an NEA grant, the Pirate's Alley Faulkner Gold Prize in the Novel, the Mid-List First Series Award, and others—and she's received a number of residency fellowships, including a stay at the Moulin à Nef in Auvillar, France. She contributes irregularly to the *New York Times* and for many years was a regular blogger at *Lingua Franca*.

Foreign Climes is the 2020 winner of the Brighthorse Prize in Short Fiction.